Table of Contents

.... 1
Backrooms: No Way Out...........
I made it..................................
Urban Exploring.......................
First Look................................
Going in...................................
The Door .... ̣2
Was it Two or Three Lights? 14
Rooms 16
Pee Break 18
The next day and the next..... 20
VAMPIRE WATER FOUNTAIN 22
Newspaper... 24
Testing... 26
Private Smith 28
Vampire Bites.. 30
Leveled Up! 32
Same surroundings, better coffee 34
Up up and Away.. 36
Not so Fast 38
Tall Man 39
Doors... 40
Invisible People 42
No More Clues... 44
Mostly Better Now 46
Recovery 48
The Briefcase 49
Alex Z%#$% 51
Three months to live 53
Going Back 55
Backrooms: Beginnings.. 57

Dr Z 58

Interview 59

Dr C 60

The BackOffices 61

17 62

5 Minutes 64

Time Travel 65

Profits 66

Paradox 68

New Approach 69

Going In 70

Copy 72

Murder 74

Not The First Time 76

Welcome Back 77

New Backrooms 79

Pigs 80

Dead Pigs 81

Smiths 83

Small, Medium, and Large Smiths 84

Let the Betting Begin 85

Jesus Smith 86

Rinse and Repeat 87

Hiking 88

Biking 89

Motorcycling 90

A New Universe 92

I Know Them! 94

Personal Life 96

Playing it Safe 97

Floating 99

Flying 100

Same Place 101

Traps 102

Surprise Attack.. 104

How Many More 106

A Year Lost... 108

Homecoming.. 110

1 Year Later 111

2 Years Later... 112

5 Years Later... 113

10 Years Later 114

20 Years Later 116

Backrooms: No Way Out

I made it

I'm not a writer or that great of a storyteller, but this is my journey into the "Backrooms." Yes, I did make it out, missing a finger and an ear. I just wanted to write all this stuff down before I figure out what to do next.

The address I have leads me to a scientist's house. I'm not sure if he's alive anymore, perhaps it's his grandson or granddaughter, or maybe just someone who knows something. It's not much to go off, but I've arrived at the doorstep. I hope someone is home because I really need to talk to someone. I've been walking for hours, and exhaustion is beginning to take its toll. Finding a place to rest for the night has become a priority, though I'm uncertain about my next steps.

Whatever awaits behind this door, be it human or otherwise, they have some explaining to do about what I just went through. I would also like to know who has my ear!

In preparation for any potential outcomes, I've sent my journal to my friend Rhonda, instructing her to give it to the police if she doesn't hear back from me. This journal contains my account of the twisted reality I either escaped from or may still be trapped within. It's my hope that these notes will serve as a guide for anyone who finds themselves in a similar situation, increasing their chances of survival and preserving their well-being.

Standing before the scientist's door, I feel a mix of anticipation and anxiety coursing through my weary body. The address on the tattered paper in my pocket matches the one etched on the door. The house itself appears weathered, its exterior bearing the marks of time's passage. Chipped paint and grimy windows give off an air of abandonment.

Hesitant yet determined, I pause for a moment to gather my thoughts. The journey so far has left me exhausted and on edge, but I must press forward. I take a deep breath, summoning my remaining courage, and decide to wait at the door instead of knocking.

The silence weighs heavily upon me as I stand there, the weight of my experiences in the "Backrooms" still fresh in my mind. Questions and uncertainties swirl within me, each demanding answers I hope to find behind this door. But for now, I can only wait, hoping that someone will emerge, ready to listen and offer guidance.

As time passes, the old house remains still, its secrets locked away. The sun casts long shadows through the cracks in the door, and the world outside carries on, oblivious to the turmoil dwelling within me.

Urban Exploring

When I moved to New York, I picked up a new hobby called Urban Exploring; that's when you head out to abandoned buildings or crawl through old underground passages. I was always fascinated by the decaying remnants and hidden secrets that lurked within the city. The allure of exploring abandoned buildings and navigating forgotten tunnels enticed me. I would spend countless hours venturing into every nook and cranny, driven by the thrill of uncovering the next hidden entrance or stumbling upon a forgotten room with stories to tell.

Urban exploring was not without its risks, though. The abandoned buildings often harbored dangers such as asbestos and the growth of unknown substances in the cold, damp, rotting structures. But for me, the risks were worth it. It was a way to gain a deeper appreciation for urban decay, to witness the history that had been left behind.

In a city like New York, there was no shortage of places to explore and secrets to uncover. Locations like Dead Horse Beach, Roosevelt Island Smallpox Hospital, and Fort Tilden were just a few of the intriguing spots waiting to be discovered. However, one of my absolute favorites was the Freedom Tunnel. Stretching for about three miles, this underground passage attracted numerous explorers, both for its historical significance and its allure as a popular spot for illicit activities or graffiti art. Its walls were often adorned with political statements, humorous graffiti, and declarations of love, reflecting the ever-changing societal sentiments.

Deep within the tunnel, about halfway through, there was a spot that caught my attention. It appeared to be an old Coke advertisement, harkening back to the 1950s. Despite multiple attempts to cover it up, the faint outlines of the vintage ad remained, giving it a ghostly presence amidst the layers of spray-painted art and scribbled messages. Determined to capture this unique find, I carefully climbed up onto a nearby beam, seeking the perfect angle for my photo.

With my camera poised, I squeezed through a small rectangular opening in the wall, only large enough for a ten-year-old to fit through. It was dark inside, and I relied on the dim light filtering through the tunnel to guide my way. As I maneuvered through the tight space, I couldn't help but feel a sense of excitement mingled with unease. The air smelled musty, tainted with hints of dampness and decay.

Eventually, I found myself in a small chamber, the remnants of an old water drainage system, I presumed. The beam I had climbed up on was to my left, and the rectangular opening I had crawled through was directly above it. I carefully balanced myself, capturing the image of the vintage Coke advertisement on my camera, hoping to share it with others and preserve this piece of forgotten history.Rhonda: The picture that I took is on my desktop. Print that out and show it to the police or whoever you give this to. It's not that easy to find in the dark but the photo will help. The beam is to your left and the opening is right above it. I think it was for water drainage or something else (yuck).

First Look

I poked my head through the opening along with my flashlight. The one thing I didn't see on the other side was the usual spray paint. I didn't even see any cans or litter; this was virgin territory! I'm not too sure how this area was never explored but my heart started to race imagining what treasures were on the other side. You always hear about explorers in Colorado finding old Levis left behind by miners worth hundreds of dollars. Maybe I can find, well, I don't know, something. Anyway, adventure awaits! But, man, I'm getting hungry, and I need to get some fresh batteries...I've learned my lesson a few times; always have backup batteries. Yet, I guess I didn't really learn that lesson because, well, here I am (again).

Rhonda: Put in a note to tell the police not to rely on their phone as a flashlight because when they are in the tunnel, the phone starts to roam, sucking all the battery life quickly. Tell them they need to get a real flashlight, the kind that I have, that you can wear on your forehead to keep your hands free.

Leaving the tunnel entrance behind for the time being, I headed back to my apartment to gather the necessary supplies. With fresh batteries and a stash of Cliff bars in my backpack, I felt a renewed sense of anticipation. An all-night exploration adventure awaited me, and I was determined to make the most of it.

As I prepared to venture back into the unknown, the thought of what awaited me in that untouched portion of the tunnel sparked a mix of curiosity and exhilaration. What hidden wonders lay hidden within those unexplored depths? It was the thrill of the unknown that fueled my passion for urban exploration, the desire to uncover the forgotten stories and forgotten artifacts that whispered through the echoes of time.

Armed with a renewed sense of purpose, I shouldered my backpack, ensuring I had all the essentials for a night filled with adventure. The tunnel beckoned, its mysteries calling out to me. With each step I took towards its mouth, I couldn't help but feel a surge of adrenaline, knowing that this journey would bring me closer to the truth of the Backrooms.

Little did I know that this particular expedition would mark a turning point in my life, unraveling a series of events that would challenge my perceptions of reality and test the limits of my courage. The first glimpse into that untouched section of the tunnel was merely the beginning, a glimpse into a world that defied logic and reason.

With a mix of excitement and trepidation, I stepped back into the darkness, ready to embrace the unknown and unveil the secrets that awaited me within the depths of the Tunnel.

Going in

I waited until dark to go back in, I didn't want anyone else to explore my untouched area before I got the opportunity to explore it all by myself.

Rhonda: I think I was in there for a month because I called you right after I got out and went to the hospital. I swear it only felt like a week but with no windows or much of anything, I couldn't keep track of the time after my phone died. Rhonda, tell them to wear a watch or something because there is just something weird with how time works in there.

My heart raced, fueled by a mix of anticipation and trepidation, as I finally mustered up the courage to enter the room beyond the narrow entrance. Like a sausage being squeezed into a casing, I maneuvered my way through the small opening, feeling the darkness engulf me as I left the tunnel behind. In the absence of light, my surroundings became an impenetrable void, leaving me disoriented and relying solely on my instincts to guide me.

Slowly, inch by inch, I navigated the rectangular passage, feeling the weight of the cramped space pressing against me. With each exhaled breath, I barely managed to wriggle my way through the tight fit. It was a struggle that seemed to stretch on for what felt like an eternity, a battle against the lack of oxygen threatening to overtake me. My body strained under the duress, and I feared that I might succumb to unconsciousness. Yet, driven by sheer willpower, I persisted, inching closer to the other side until finally, I emerged into the room beyond, gasping for air.

As I stood upright, a wave of astonishment washed over me. The room was empty and untouched, a stark contrast to the decay and neglect that permeated the rest of the Backrooms. There was no trace of dust or cobwebs; it appeared as if someone had meticulously cleaned the space, as if maintaining it on a weekly basis. The eerie ambiance intensified as I realized that it was not merely quiet, but utterly silent. The usual cacophony of the bustling city was nonexistent within these walls, amplifying the sense of detachment from reality.

The room itself measured approximately ten feet by ten feet, its bare walls enclosing an atmosphere of mystery. In the corner, I noticed a solitary wastepaper basket, its presence feeling out of place amidst the emptiness. Adjacent to it stood a dark wooden door, its silent invitation beckoning me to explore further. Disappointment welled up within me as I pondered the possibility that my grand adventure had led me to nothing more than a mundane janitor's closet or an inconsequential office space.

Sighing in resignation, I decided to investigate the room in search of any clues that might shed light on its purpose. I approached the wastepaper basket, hoping to find remnants that would reveal the nature of this mysterious place. However, much like the surrounding area, the basket held only a scant offering—a folded-up newspaper resting within its confines.

Intrigued, I picked up the newspaper, unfolding its pages with anticipation. Yet, to my surprise, the newspaper was entirely blank, devoid of any articles, pictures, or text. Instead, faint outlines indicated where content should have been, ghostly remnants of information that had long since faded away. Strangely, the only discernible detail was the date—September 1, 1939—an eerily significant moment in history.

Puzzled, I carefully stowed the enigmatic newspaper in my backpack, feeling a mixture of reluctance and curiosity as I did so. It went against my personal code as an explorer to take anything from the places I visited, respecting the integrity and history of these forgotten spaces. However, in this peculiar room, where silence reigned supreme and the ordinary seemed extraordinary, I convinced myself that nobody within this empty office would miss their blank newspaper.

Little did I know that this seemingly innocuous act of taking the newspaper would set in motion a series of events that would shatter my perceptions of reality and plunge me further into the enigmatic depths of the Backrooms.

The Door

Disappointed by the seemingly mundane janitor's closet, I mustered the courage to try the door. The prospect of squeezing my way back through the narrow rectangular opening held little appeal, and I hoped that the door would offer a more straightforward exit. As I stood before it, a sense of dread gripped me, fueled by the fear of being caught or encountering something worse within the depths of this unknown place.

It was late at night, and I assumed that nobody would be working at this hour. Yet, a tinge of apprehension lingered as I considered the possibility of stumbling upon an unexpected presence behind the door. To assess the situation, I pressed my ear against the wooden surface, hoping to discern any signs of activity. However, all that greeted my senses was a deep, monotonous buzzing emanating from the other side. It reverberated through the door, filling the air with an unrelenting drone.

I stood there for a few minutes, entranced by the persistent buzzing that seemed to permeate the very fabric of the room. The thought of enduring such a sound on a daily basis, should one work in this office, was disconcerting. I couldn't help but imagine how the constant buzz could gradually chip away at one's sanity or infiltrate their dreams with nightmarish visions of killer bees. I had a 50-50 chance on whether or not the door was locked. I put my ear up to the wooden door first to see if I could hear anyone, but I could just hear deep buzzing coming from the other side. I stood there for a few minutes but nothing but the drone of the buzzing. I kept thinking that if I worked here, it would drive me crazy. I bet that listening to that buzz for eight hours a day would slowly eat away your sanity or make you have killer bee nightmares.

Rhonda: Hey, why don't you write down that **ear plugs** in the backrooms are a must! Listening to that buzz 24 hours a day for a month does get you a little crazy!

When I convinced myself that nobody was on the other side, I twisted the doorknob. It was unlocked but I had to do two full turns before I could open the door. How inefficient! Maybe that's how old locks worked in the 30's, I wondered. As I opened the door the piss yellow color of the fluorescent lights filled the janitor's closet. It took my eyes a few seconds to adjust to the glare of this new color that filled the room. Now I had to deal with both the garish color and the buzzing. I felt like I was trapped in a giant bug zapper. I guess that I was lucky to only have two senses on high alert. At least it didn't smell like urine or citronella...yet.

I poked my head into the hallway and listened again, still nothing, just buzzing. I looked left and then right and did it again. While there was a light above my head, I could only see about twenty feet on either side of me. It appeared the darkness was pushing back the light; it wouldn't let it shine the rest of the way. The darkness felt heavy and so did my breathing. I felt a sense of dread.

Was it Two or Three Lights?

As I quietly crept into the hallway, I felt a squish under my feet and then a gross sort of wetness. I stupidly closed the door behind me, cementing my month-long journey. Thankfully, after a few more steps, the carpet began to dry out. The air also felt heavy and damp near the door but also seemed to dry out just like the carpet. I don't know how to describe the smell; it was stale like mothballs. Figuring that the exit would be close to the end of the hallway, I decided to veer left. If I was wrong, I could simply turn around and go the other way. Passing under two more loudly buzzing lights, I finally made it to the end of the hallway. I hoped it wouldn't be the end of me.

I looked left and then right. It was an identical setup but this room without the door. The lights gave off more of a buzzing drone than light because I still couldn't see the end of the room. Discouraged, I turned around and went back the other way. There should be a red exit glow around here somewhere. But where? Once again, I passed under two more dim, loud lights. Looking carefully left and right, I still could see no end in sight. F-this I muttered as I returned to the door. I'll squeeze myself back through the opening and forget this boring place.

I passed under two lights and then a third, but no door. I went under another light, thinking I miscounted, but I knew that I couldn't have been off more than one light. That was four lights. I just kept turning around, confused. Did I blink when I was passing the door? Am I just turned around? Is my imagination running wild? Maybe I just didn't see it. I went under one, two, three, four lights still no door or end of the long, narrow corridor.

I went under six lights until I reached the end of the passage. Is the hallway growing or am I just really bad at counting? This can't be right! I turned back around and surprised myself as I took off running towards the other end of the corridor. Eight lights this time. I stopped and sat down to catch my breath. None of this was making any sense.

14

Was I hallucinating? Taking a sip out my water bottle, it dawned on me. There must be a gas leak in the office and it's causing me to be confused.

As I jumped up and took off running, I ran erratically. Another right and then a left. Then a left or maybe a right again. I wanted to get away from the gas as fast as possible. I was scared and worried and out of breath (and also out of shape, I muttered). I stopped and looked back, I realized I wasn't dizzy or confused. There seemed to be no gas leak. I was lost—lost in the backrooms of a terribly- designed office building.

"Getting out should be easy," I whispered to myself. Trying to convince myself that I'll see the red glow of an exit sign around the next corner, I was devastated when it wasn't there. I raced around the next corner and the next...and the next. For several hours, I felt like a lab rat, searching for the exit. Turn after turn, I was getting more desperate and frantic.

Rooms

After what felt like an eternity of aimless wandering through the winding hallways, I finally came across a room. Each hallway I traversed consisted of four buzzing lights and identical plain square rooms on either side. These rooms mirrored the size of the janitor's closet I had initially encountered, measuring ten feet by ten feet. However, they were devoid of any objects or signs of life, maintaining an eerie emptiness.

As I moved from one room to the next, an overwhelming sense of monotony settled over me. The repetition became disheartening, like a cruel loop that refused to release its grip. The relentless sameness amplified my feelings of entrapment within this perplexing realm. Every room held the same barrenness, an emptiness that seemed to reflect the void within my own soul.

Amidst the mundane surroundings, I noticed a subtle shift in the soundscape. The constant buzzing of the lights had evolved into a low, persistent hum. Whether it was due to my ears becoming accustomed to the incessant noise or a change in the auditory fabric of the Backrooms, I couldn't say. Yet, this "different" sound provided a modicum of relief, a departure from the monotonous buzzing that had plagued my senses for hours on end.

Further on, I observed another glimmer of change. The carpet beneath my feet, which had previously appeared untouched and immaculate, now revealed faint traces of wear and tear. Hints of where office chairs had rolled back and forth and indentations left by desks that had long since vanished were etched into the carpet's surface. It was a subtle but significant deviation from the perfect emptiness that had characterized this enigmatic place.

In the midst of my weariness and frustration, these minor variations brought a glimmer of hope. They served as reminders that within the seemingly unchanging repetition, there still existed subtle nuances, small deviations that hinted at the possibility of discovery and escape.

Driven by a renewed sense of determination, I pressed forward, my footsteps echoing through the silent hallways. Each step was infused with a desperate longing to find an exit, to break free from the clutches of this endless cycle. Although the path ahead remained uncertain and the prospect of escape elusive, I refused to succumb to the stifling monotony that threatened to consume me.

Pee Break

The pressing need for a bathroom in the Backrooms became increasingly overwhelming. How could an office building lack such a basic necessity? Frustration and discomfort coursed through me as I realized I had no viable options for relieving myself. The dwindling contents of my water bottle offered no relief.

Desperation led me into one of the empty rooms, where I found myself contemplating the most undignified options for addressing my bodily functions. Should I attempt to use the water bottle, find a discreet corner, or lean against a wall? The lack of any suitable facilities forced me to consider unorthodox choices in this surreal and unwelcoming place.

Paranoia gripped me as I weighed the potential consequences of being caught in the act. Though the Backrooms appeared devoid of any other living souls, I couldn't shake the nagging fear of surveillance or an unexpected encounter. The thought of being apprehended and facing legal consequences for trespassing sent chills down my spine. Anxious thoughts swirled in my mind, imagining unseen eyes watching my every move.

Trying to regain a sense of rationality, I chided myself for succumbing to irrational fears. It was unlikely that anyone would stumble upon me in this desolate maze. Yet, the persistent hum of unease refused to dissipate. The absence of visible cameras or signs of surveillance provided some relief, but paranoia still clung to my thoughts.

The eerie notion of an unfortunate security guard, bored and tasked with monitoring my every move, sent shivers down my spine. But a glimmer of hope emerged as I considered the possibility that the end of their shift might bring rescue from this disorienting labyrinth. Was it too much to wish for a guardian angel to lead me out of this bizarre realm?

Scanning the room, I found no evidence of cameras, not even hidden within the now humming, pee-yellow lights that bathed the space. Desperation continued to cloud my judgment, intensifying with each passing moment. Exhaustion had taken hold of me more deeply than I had realized, and I succumbed to a fitful slumber, oblivious to the dire situation surrounding me. Apparently, I was even more exhausted than I realized. I guess that I succumbed to the exhaustion because I woke up way too close to my pee puddle. Gross.

Suppressing the embarrassment and the need for cleanliness, I forced myself to rise, determined to push forward in my search for an exit. The urgency of escaping the clutches of the Backrooms propelled me forward, despite the discomfort and the ever-growing challenges that lay ahead.

The next day and the next....

Days had blurred into each other within the desolate corridors of the Backrooms. The meager sustenance provided by my Cliff bars had long been depleted, and not a drop of water remained. A heavy sigh escaped my parched lips as worry gnawed at my insides. This was the first time I had gone without food or water for an entire day, and the reality of my situation began to weigh heavily upon me.

Initially, the absence of nourishment didn't seem too dire. I reasoned that if there were countless individuals in the world forced to endure hunger, I could endure it too. After all, I was relatively healthy. But as time wore on, the effects of dehydration and hunger started to take their toll. Two days, or maybe it was merely ten hours, into this ordeal, I could no longer dismiss the discomfort.

Rhonda's reminder about the importance of a watch echoed in my mind. The watch, with its hands and proximity to the hand, became a symbol of timekeeping and a vital tool in this surreal realm. Its presence would have provided me with a sense of structure, a means to track the passage of time. I regretted not having one at my disposal.

Slowing my pace, I couldn't help but notice the distinct marks etched into the carpet beneath my weary feet. Lines and indentations revealed the former presence of desks, chairs, and cabinets. Even the walls bore faint remnants of where pictures once adorned their bland surfaces. My mind wandered, envisioning the generic images that might have hung on these walls—endless scenes of water, from serene lakes to babbling streams, a constant reminder of what I craved the most.

Suddenly, hope sparked within me as I turned the corner and laid my eyes upon a water fountain. It stood there, an oasis amidst the barren surroundings, its presence both tantalizing and perplexing. Could it be real? Or was it merely a mirage, a cruel illusion conjured by the depths of this enigmatic place?

Cautiously, I approached the water fountain, my steps hesitant yet filled with desperate anticipation. The sight of running water ignited a primal thirst within me, a yearning for something to quench the parched desert that my mouth had become. A flicker of hope mingled with skepticism, unsure of what awaited me as I drew closer.

Reaching out, my trembling hand hesitantly pressed against the cool metal of the fountain's button. I held my breath, hoping against hope that the rush of water would soon gush forth, offering relief to my parched tongue.

BEWARE VAMPIRE WATER FOUNTAIN

My desperation propelled me towards the water fountain, my heart racing with anticipation. I pressed on the round silver button, and with a surge of relief, water sputtered out. However, my relief was short-lived as an unexpected jolt of pain shot through my finger. Confusion and frustration gripped me as I examined the button, searching for anything that could have caused the sharp sensation. To my dismay, there seemed to be no visible source of harm.

Blood trickled from my injured finger, dampening my hopes of quenching my thirst. Determined not to let this setback deter me, I hastily wrapped my shirt around my finger as a makeshift barrier, attempting to protect myself from any unseen sharp edges. With a renewed sense of desperation, I pressed the button once more, but to no avail. Despite exerting more force, the water refused to flow.

In a moment of sheer desperation, I discarded caution and pressed my bare finger against the button, bracing myself for the anticipated pain. Water erupted from the fountain, accompanied by an intense surge of agony in my finger. The pain was excruciating, but my thirst overpowered any rational thought. Bent over, I greedily gulped down the water, allowing brief respite from the torment.

After taking a few desperate sips, the pain became unbearable. I looked down at my finger, now swollen and discolored, an ominous sign of a deeper wound. Fear surged through me as I hastily tore off a piece of my shirt, using it as a makeshift bandage to stave off further damage. Reluctantly, I distanced myself from the treacherous water fountain, unwilling to witness the full extent of the harm it had inflicted upon me.

Lost and disheartened, I found myself sitting helplessly beside the water fountain, contemplating my next move. Should I attempt to drink more, risking further injury? Or should I continue my journey through the labyrinthine hallways in search of an escape? The uncertainty weighed heavily upon me as time stretched on.

Fatigue eventually overcame me, and I drifted into a restless slumber. Hours later, a sharp pang of pain roused me from my sleep. The condition of my injured finger had worsened, serving as a harsh reminder of the perils lurking within this mysterious place. I berated myself mentally, vowing to exercise greater caution in the future.

Gazing upon the seemingly innocent water fountain once more, I could discern nothing out of the ordinary. Its plain appearance belied the danger it concealed, an unassuming trap for the unwary. With a mix of trepidation and determination, I rose from my spot and made a silent vow to steer clear of the wicked water fountain. There was still much to explore, and my survival depended on navigating this bizarre world with caution and vigilance. I looked over the fountain again and saw nothing out of the ordinary, just a plain water fountain that bites.

Newspaper

Man, my legs were tired. Everything about me was tired. I felt zombielike. As I sat and stared at the wall, I was numb. I didn't even want to think about anything, yet I kept wondering how I got myself into this mess. Exhaustion weighed heavily upon me, my legs still aching and my entire being enveloped in weariness. I felt like a mere shell of myself, moving through the Backrooms with a zombie-like demeanor. Numbness settled over me as I sat against the wall, my thoughts drifting aimlessly. The weight of my predicament pressed upon me, and despite my reluctance, I couldn't help but ponder how I had ended up in this bewildering maze.

In an attempt to distract my weary mind, I reached into my backpack and retrieved the newspaper. Unfolding it, I was greeted by a change in the date—September 10, 1939. The realization struck me with a mix of confusion and dread. Had I truly been trapped within these walls for ten days? The articles and pictures on the newspaper's pages seemed slightly more discernible, but my tired, dry eyes struggled to make out the details.

A sense of frustration washed over me as I contemplated how many more days it might take before I could fully read and understand the contents of the newspaper. I wondered how many more days it would take before I would be able to read the newspaper. Maybe ten more days? Unless, of course, I had already succumbed to the clutches of this eerie realm. The thought sent a chill down my spine, disbelief mingling with a newfound fear. Had I been so blind to the potential dangers lurking within the backrooms? The realization dawned upon me—my life was at stake, would I still be alive in ten days?

Shaking my head in an attempt to dispel the overwhelming shock, I was overcome by an urgency to escape. This bizarre world, trapped within the confines of an abandoned office building, had taken its toll on my psyche. The mere idea of perishing in this forsaken place felt unfathomable. I couldn't succumb to despair; I had to find a way out.

Summoning the last remnants of determination, I pushed myself to my feet. Weariness clung to me, like an unwelcome companion, but I refused to let it consume me. With each step forward, I vowed to keep pushing, to remain vigilant against the perils that lay in wait within the depths of the Backrooms. My quest for escape had taken on a renewed sense of urgency—a burning desire to break free from the confines of this twisted reality and return to the world of the living. Unless of course I'm already dead, I thought. It never occurred to me that I might die in here, in the backrooms of an abandoned office building. How messed up is that? I was in a state of shock. I had to get out, I had to get out of here.

Testing

The hallways stretched endlessly before me, each turn blending into the next, a maze of confusion and frustration. Left, right, left, left, right—I had lost count of the countless turns I had taken. It seemed that no matter which path I chose, the outcome remained the same. This place defied logic, mocking my attempts to find a way out. Why bother? It all seemed so futile.

Seeking some semblance of order amidst the chaos, I embarked on a three-hour journey taking only right turns. Did it lead me back to where I started? I couldn't say for certain. Then, in a desperate attempt to break free from the monotony, I repeated the process, this time opting for left turns. Did it yield a different outcome? Once again, I found myself unable to provide a definitive answer.

Memories of a movie I had watched during my younger years resurfaced—a tale of survivors stranded in a desert after a plane crash. One of the survivors, determined to find help, was cautioned that their journey would likely lead them in a circle due to the uneven strength of their legs. Could I be trapped in a similar predicament? Was I unwittingly walking in a grand, repetitive loop, a meditative maze with no escape?

Recalling the movie's ending proved challenging, my fragmented memory offering no clear resolution. All I could grasp was the glimmer of hope that the survivors had been rescued. Clinging to that sliver of optimism, I questioned what I could do in my own dire situation.

An idea struck me—I decided to remove my left shoe, hoping that it would help balance my steps. The relief was instantaneous, and I marveled at the newfound equilibrium. Testing my theory, I walked down the hallway, this time remaining more centered. To my surprise, the inevitable collision with the right-side wall was avoided, and I smoothly turned the corner, continuing my journey down another passage.

Curiosity piqued, I repeated the process, this time removing my right shoe. With each step, I positioned myself towards the middle of the hallway. Astonishingly, the pattern held true—I was drawn towards the right side, brushing against the wall. A growing realization dawned upon me, though I struggled to comprehend its full implications.

Standing in the corridor, I examined its structure more closely. It was then that I noticed a subtle bend—a slight curvature to the left. It became evident that this distortion persisted regardless of the path I took. Whether I turned left or right, I was destined to walk in a circle, perpetually retracing my steps.

A mixture of frustration and acceptance welled up within me. How long had I been trapped in this circular labyrinth? The realization settled heavily upon my weary shoulders. My efforts, however valiant, were in vain. The very essence of this place conspired against my escape, forcing me into an eternal cycle.

Yet, amid the suffocating confines of this infinite loop, a flicker of determination ignited within me. I refused to surrender to this cruel fate. I would continue to explore, to seek any glimmer of hope, even in the face of futility. For as long as I had breath in my lungs and the will to endure, I would strive to find a way out of this nightmarish purgatory.

Private Smith

I turned a corner and "met" Private Smith for the first time. Smith was in a yellow hazmat suit, and he was sticking out of a wall about five feet in the air. The only visible parts of Smith was the upper half of his body. There was a rope that appeared to be tied around him that vanished into the wall just like the rest of his body. The only label on the yellow hazmat suit said *Private Smith*. There weren't any other clues as to what Smith was doing there protruding through the wall. The markings on the wall told the story of how Smith appeared to be trapped for several days. It looked like he tried to punch and claw his way out, but yet, there he remained, stuck in the wall dead, like a mounted hunting trophy.

I walked over to Private Smith and took a look in the visor of his suit, the best description I can make was Private Smith was now a human soup. An eyeball floated by which sealed the deal on whether or not I was going to open the hazmat suit to see if I could find anything useful.

In the days that followed, my journey through the eerie corridors of the Backrooms led me to discover more fragments of Private Smith. It seemed as though his presence was scattered throughout the maze-like passages, a chilling reminder of the fate that awaited those who delved too deeply into this strange realm.

As I navigated the labyrinthine corridors, I would occasionally come across arms, legs, and torsos, all encased within the familiar yellow hazmat suits. They were eerily trapped within the walls, their limbs seemingly melding with the solid structure. The sight sent shivers down my spine, as if the very essence of Private Smith had become intertwined with the Backrooms themselves.

In some instances, I encountered fragments of Private Smith in even more bizarre locations. There were instances where his limbs protruded from the ceiling, as if he had been forcefully pushed through the solid surface above. The sight of hands and legs hanging down from above, suspended in mid-air, added another layer of dread to the already unnerving atmosphere of the Backrooms.

But perhaps the most unsettling encounters were those where Private Smith appeared to emerge from the floors, his body partially submerged within the solid ground. It was as though the very fabric of the Backrooms had absorbed his form, leaving him forever trapped between the boundaries of reality and this inexplicable dimension.

As I observed these fragmented forms of Private Smith, I couldn't help but wonder what had led to their gruesome fate. What series of events had unfolded to scatter his remains throughout the Backrooms? It was a mystery that deepened with each new encounter, as the pieces of the puzzle refused to align, leaving me with more questions than answers.

Yet, despite the chilling presence of Private Smith's fragmented remains, I remained determined to forge ahead, to find a way out of this sinister realm. The sight of his scattered body parts served as a constant reminder of the perils that lurked within the depths of the Backrooms, urging me to remain vigilant and cautious.

With each passing encounter, the puzzle of Private Smith grew, casting a shadow over my own journey through the Backrooms. I couldn't help but wonder what had truly become of him. Was he a victim of the Backrooms, forever trapped within its distorted reality? Or was there a glimmer of hope that he had found a way to escape, leaving behind only traces of his harrowing journey?

As I ventured deeper into the treacherous corridors, the mystery of Private Smith became a haunting presence, an unsolved riddle that fueled both my fear and my determination to find an exit from this unfathomable realm. The last time I found anything about Smith was a discarded fully complete top and bottom yellow suit. Congratulations Private Smith for making it out of the wall, I wonder if you ever made it out of the Backrooms.

Vampire Bites

I made a decision to leave markers behind as I ventured through the seemingly endless corridors of the Backrooms. With every turn I took, I scratched the walls, hoping to create a trail that would lead me back to familiar territory. But to my dismay, I never stumbled upon those marks again. It was as if the walls themselves shifted and erased any trace of my presence, leaving me disoriented and lost.

Though I couldn't determine the exact size of the circle I was trapped in, I knew with certainty that I was indeed trapped in a circular path. The relentless repetition of hallways and turns confirmed this unsettling reality. Was I stuck in the center, endlessly circling around, or was I caught on the outer edge, forever reaching for an escape that remained just out of reach? The answer eluded me, adding to the growing frustration and despair that consumed my mind.

Meanwhile, my injured finger continued to deteriorate. I encountered the vampire water fountain on two more occasions, each time sacrificing a different finger to its treacherous bite. The first finger I used had turned black, devoid of any sensation. The other two fingers had turned an unsettling shade of blue, a grim reminder of the toll the Backrooms were taking on my physical well-being. And to my surprise, one of those fingers eventually fell off, lost to the cruel grasp of this nightmarish realm. The missing ear was another peculiar tale, one that offered a brief moment of amusement amidst the prevailing gloom.

As I continued to consult the newspaper, the date now reading September 20th, 1939, the outside world felt like a distant memory. The news of the ongoing World War, the updates on the Yankees' season, and the forecast of rain tomorrow served as a stark contrast to the surreal existence within the Backrooms. It was a disconcerting reminder of the disconnect between the outside world and this twisted dimension I found myself trapped in.

In an act of frustration and defiance, I approached the vampire water fountain once more, filled with resentment towards the pain and suffering it had caused me. With a surge of anger, I ran towards it and kicked it with all my might. The fountain toppled over, crashing against the ground, and water burst forth freely into the air. I quickly seized the opportunity, using my empty water bottle to collect as much water as I could. It was a moment of triumph, a small victory in the face of adversity. But what truly brought a smile to my face wasn't just the precious water I now possessed—it was the revelation that the fallen fountain had revealed a hidden hole in the wall, previously obscured by its presence. Perhaps, just perhaps, this newfound opening would lead me closer to the escape I desperately sought.

Leveled Up!

As I squeezed myself through the hole in the wall, I couldn't help but notice how much weight I had lost during my time in the Backrooms. The lack of hunger and the strange energy that coursed through me defied all logic. I should have withered away by now, succumbing to the deprivation of food and water. Yet, here I was, feeling surprisingly agile and revitalized. Time in this place seemed to bend and distort, refusing to conform to the laws of the outside world.

Using a nearby water pipe, I hoisted myself up between the walls, ascending about ten feet until I reached the back of another fountain. With a burst of adrenaline, I delivered a powerful Kung Fu kick that sent the fountain flying across the room. I swung out and eagerly gulped down as much water as I could before it ceased to flow.

A sudden gasp escaped my lips as I struggled to comprehend the reality of the situation. I must be dreaming, I told myself repeatedly, desperately trying to convince myself that this newfound oasis was nothing more than a figment of my imagination. Despite my doubts, I rushed over to the counter and pressed the button on the coffee machine, fully expecting it to yield no result. But to my astonishment, a stream of extra bold coffee poured into the waiting cup, followed by a generous amount of sugar and cream. It was surreal, yet undeniably real. I sat down and savored every sip, relishing in the taste of the best coffee I had ever experienced.

My eyes then fell upon a vending machine nearby, its glass shattered but its contents still intact. With a sense of fortune, I managed to salvage a couple of stale Baby Ruth candy bars, savoring their nostalgic sweetness as I indulged in this unexpected treat.

Looking around the room, I couldn't shake the feeling that someone else had been here before me. Could it have been Private Smith? Did he discover the hidden passage behind one of the fountains? There were no immediate signs of another presence, but the thought of encountering another human, whether friendly or not, filled me with a sense of longing. After four cups of coffee and a couple of well-deserved bathroom breaks, I felt a renewed determination to explore my newfound surroundings. Confidence in my ability to find an escape began to flicker back to life, illuminating a glimmer of hope in the darkness of the Backrooms.

Same surroundings, better coffee

As I continued to explore this level of the Backrooms, a disheartening sameness engulfed me. The curved hallways, the relentless hum of the yellow lights, and the once-empty rooms now filled with vacant desks and chairs—they all blended into a monotonous tapestry. Desperation gnawed at me as I searched for any sign or clue that could lead me to an escape. I rifled through the desks, hoping to find a hidden message or a map, but my efforts yielded nothing. Even sitting in the chairs and spinning around in a futile attempt to break the cycle proved fruitless.

Frustration and fatigue consumed me, but I couldn't give up. The only thing that had produced any kind of result in this surreal realm was a forceful kick to the water fountain. So, I pondered, what else could I kick? Another vending machine caught my attention, and without hesitation, I delivered a swift kick to its side. To my disappointment, only a few more candy bars and coins tumbled out, scattering across the floor. My backpack was already overflowing with candy bars, so I left the scattered treats behind. However, I couldn't help but notice that all the coins had rolled to one side of the break room.

Curiosity piqued, I picked up one of the coins and placed it in the center of the room. With a flick of my finger, I set it spinning like a top. To my astonishment, the coin gradually veered toward the side of the room where the rest of the coins had gathered. It was as if an invisible force was pulling them in that direction. As I surveyed the room once more, I began to discern a subtle difference—one side of the room was slightly elevated compared to the other. It was a barely noticeable incline, but now that I had recognized it, I couldn't unsee it.

Stepping out into the hallway, I observed the same phenomenon. The hallways, which had previously seemed straight, now revealed their slight bend to the left. And at one end, there was a subtle elevation, barely perceptible to the naked eye. A surge of hope swelled within me.

Could this irregularity be the key to finding an exit? With newfound determination, I resolved to explore further, following the path that led me to the higher side of the hallway. Perhaps, just perhaps, this discovery would be the breakthrough I desperately needed.

Up up and Away

With a newfound sense of purpose, I ascended further into the labyrinthine corridors, my focus solely on reaching higher ground. The direction—left or right—no longer mattered. The only guiding principle was to follow the path that pointed upward. As I climbed, the surroundings seemed to shift. Desks and walls became adorned with various items, and faint murmurs of distant voices echoed through the air. It was as if an eerie semblance of life had seeped into this strange realm.

Occasionally, during my breaks, I would examine the papers and notebooks scattered across the desks. The writing was still too faint to decipher, reminiscent of the initial state of the newspaper I had found. Despite the effort, the words remained elusive, teasing me with their almost-decipherable presence. During these moments of respite, I would revisit the newspaper, reading and rereading the articles in the hopes of uncovering a hidden clue, but to no avail. The date on the newspaper remained unchanged, a constant reminder of the passage of time that held me captive.

The isolation and uncertainty began to take a toll on my sanity. The voice inside my head grew louder, questioning my resolve, sowing seeds of doubt and despair. It became a weight that dragged me down, threatening to plunge me into a deep abyss of darkness. Every moment of stillness intensified the struggle to keep moving forward. The mental and emotional exhaustion made it increasingly difficult to rise from each seated rest. But I knew I had to persevere. "Keep moving," I urged myself, mustering the strength to push through the overwhelming heaviness and continue my journey.

As the voice inside my head gnawed at my resolve, I clung to the flickering embers of hope that remained. I reminded myself that there had to be a way out, an escape from this suffocating maze of corridors. I couldn't let despair consume me entirely. So, with each laborious effort to rise from my temporary respite, I steeled myself and pressed onward. I had come too far to surrender to the darkness that threatened to engulf me. I had to keep moving, to continue searching for the elusive path that would lead me back to the world beyond the Backrooms.

I'm starting to lose it again, the voice inside my head tells me I am not sure if I can do it. I am not sure if I want to do it, I am not sure if I can live. The voice keeps growing louder and louder, acting as a weight, pulling my sanity down to a deep dark place the longer I'm lost in here.

Every time I sat down it was so much harder to get back up. Keep moving I told myself, get back up and keep moving.

Not so Fast

I was almost at a jogging pace before I noticed something that knocked the wind out of me. The pee yellow lights were humming a little louder, and shining brighter, I could now feel the warmth of their glow.

I looked over at the wall and I noticed the faint pictures displayed on the wall were now almost touching the ceiling. Then it hit me, the floor was going higher, but the ceiling remained the same. Who came up with such a sick tortured place? I couldn't take it anymore, so I just screamed and screamed and screamed and fell to the ground, but then, someone shouted for me to *shut up*!

I was so shocked I didn't know what to do. I stopped and stared and shouted *Hello? Who's there?*, but nothing, can you *help* me, nothing, *please* I'm lost can someone just *help* me, nothing, then from somewhere behind me I heard a door open and then shut.

I haven't seen a door since I first came here, but I heard one just now, just right around the last corner I came from. My heart raced with anticipation as a glimmer of hope flickered within me. Without hesitation, I retraced my steps, rushing back along the corridor, my anticipation growing with each passing moment. I turned the final corner, and there he stood—a figure emerging from the shadows.

In that moment, relief and disbelief intermingled within me. It had been so long since I had encountered another human being, a lifeline in this desolate expanse. Their presence brought a mixture of emotions—curiosity, gratitude, and apprehension. Who was this person? How did they come to be here? As I stood before them, the words caught in my throat, and for a moment, silence hung heavily in the air, pregnant with anticipation for the interaction that was about to unfold.

Tall Man

The Tall Man stood there, an enigma of shapelessness. His face, his body—bereft of discernible features. But one thing was undeniable: his towering height, his long limbs extending outward. And there, in his hand, a knife—ominous and foreboding.

As my eyes scanned the space, I realized the door he had emerged from had vanished. It was as if it had been swallowed by the very fabric of this strange realm. With each deliberate step, the Tall Man approached, his elongated legs moving fluidly, devoid of the natural bend of knees. In just two strides, he loomed over me, his gaze fixed upon my trembling form.

I should have been able to distinguish his facial features, to read the emotions etched upon his countenance. But his face remained an indistinct blur, as if crafted from the same ethereal matter that defined this labyrinthine nightmare. A surge of fear coursed through me, compelling me to flee. I turned to run and that's when my ear went missing, it hurt, it hurt bad, but I ran. I turned and saw the Tall man picking up my ear and wiping the blood off his knife. Then a distinctive smile appear on his face as he became to charge at me. For every six steps I took the Tall Man only had to only lurch two steps, he was very swift, but I was quicker around the turns. He would catch up with me in the hallways but at every turn I would put some distance in between us.

I kept hearing a thumping sound, once when I looked to see if he was still after me, I saw him hit his head on the ceiling. That's when I knew my only chance was to keep going up, it seemed like an eternity, but his head thumps grew more and more and eventually they started to make him lose his balance. The Tall Man finally had to slow down, and he eventually stopped all together. I heard another door open and shut behind me, I never saw the Tall Man again, so I thought.

Doors

I pushed myself to keep running, my legs carrying me forward as I propelled myself through the seemingly endless corridors. Minutes turned into what felt like an eternity, until I could no longer maintain my frantic pace. Slowing to a jog, I fought to catch my breath, my chest heaving with each gasp of air. The pain from my missing ear resurfaced, a reminder of the sacrifices made in this treacherous journey.

As I turned the corner, I was met with an unexpected obstacle—the ceiling looming perilously close. The walls were closing in, my options dwindling. Desperation welled within me, fueling my determination to find a way out. The muffled voices I had heard earlier grew louder, snippets of conversations, the clacking of typewriters, and the murmur of office meetings. I strained to make sense of the sounds, but with only one functioning ear, their meaning eluded me.

I paused, leaning against the wall, surveying the hallway before me. It curved to the left, ascending slightly, but it felt as though there must be something more, something I had overlooked. I closed my eyes, taking a deep breath, and then another. And in that moment, a subtle revelation struck me—the air. It was different here, fresher than the stale atmosphere that had plagued me throughout my journey. Determined, I ventured up and down the hallway, my senses attuned to every subtle scent.

And there it was—a cool spot on the wall, a gentle breeze whispering from within. Without hesitation, I pressed against the area, feeling the resistance give way. A door materialized before me, leading into yet another janitor's closet. My eyes were drawn to the ladder ascending towards an unknown destination. Excitement coursed through my veins as I realized this was my chance, one step closer to escaping this twisted labyrinth.

With renewed hope, I ascended the ladder, my hands gripping each rung as I climbed higher. The door closed behind me, shutting off the path that had brought me this far. It was a small victory, but it filled me with a renewed sense of purpose. Each step, each floor, brought me closer to the elusive exit that seemed to taunt me from the depths of this surreal realm.

Invisible People

I stood at the threshold of the next door, my heart pounding in anticipation. Beyond it, I could hear the faint murmur of voices, growing nearer with each passing moment. I braced myself for what lay ahead, uncertain of whether they would offer salvation or deliver me back into the clutches of the Tall Man, his knife poised for another grisly prize.

Hours ticked by as I waited, the tension mounting with each passing second. The voices gradually faded, their purpose and destination unknown. With a sense of urgency, I made the decision to venture forth, knowing that time was slipping through my fingers. Cautiously, I opened the door just a crack, peering out into the unknown.

To my surprise, the harsh yellow glow of the lights had been replaced by a softer, more welcoming fluorescent illumination. The hum persisted, but it was no longer an assault on my senses. The carpet, though worn, appeared newer, a faint sign of care in this mysterious realm. I took in the surroundings, noting the distinct shapes of the pictures adorning the walls, their nostalgic 1950s style evoking a sense of familiarity.

Moving forward with fear, I traversed the hallway, my footsteps echoing in the silence. The desks, adorned with family photographs, hinted at a semblance of normalcy. Pencils and pens lay neatly arranged, while antiquated rotary phones and typewriters adorned the surfaces. It was a scene frozen in time, a relic of a bygone era.

The break room beckoned, its aroma drawing me in. To my delight, the coffee machine awaited me, accompanied now by an array of doughnuts and fresh fruits. I indulged in the sweet and juicy offerings, savoring each bite as if it were a taste of freedom itself. However, my enjoyment was tinged with caution, as I remained ever vigilant for the return of the voices that had echoed through the corridors.

As if on cue, the sound of approaching footsteps reached my ears. Instinctively, I darted to the nearest desk, sliding beneath its sheltering surface. Peering out with bated breath, I strained to catch a glimpse of the passersby. Yet, to my surprise, I saw no one. Only the echoes of their conversations filled the air, their words tantalizingly close yet frustratingly unintelligible.

Several times, this scenario repeated itself, the voices passing by in close proximity, yet eluding my sight. I strained to comprehend their meaning, to glean any semblance of direction or purpose. Yet, each time, the voices faded into the distance, leaving me in a state of bewilderment.

Eventually, the voices dissipated entirely, swallowed by the enveloping silence. The lights dimmed, casting a veil of darkness over the corridor. I yearned to follow the path they had taken, but the hallway stretched on endlessly, offering no clear guidance. The passage of time grew shorter, and the voices would soon return, their proximity becoming an imminent threat. I could no longer hide; escape was my only recourse.

No More Clues

As I frantically searched every nook and cranny of the new level, my desperation grew. I scoured the hallways, explored every office, rifled through every desk, and even attempted to make calls on the archaic phones. Yet, my efforts proved fruitless. The elusive exit remained as elusive as ever, and I found myself no closer to escaping this enigmatic place than when I first arrived.

Frustration consumed me, and a desperate plan formed in my mind. I decided to unleash a cacophony of screams and yells, hoping that the disturbance would trigger some kind of response, opening a new door or unveiling a hidden passage. I roared with all my might, unleashing my pent-up frustration into the air. I wanted change, any change, even if it meant facing whatever they would send next. No more silent submission; if I was going down, it would be with a defiant roar.

To my astonishment, a door creaked open down the adjacent hallway. The Tall Man emerged once again, his ominous presence looming. Undeterred, I continued to scream at him, fueling my defiance with every word. In a fit of desperation, I seized a typewriter and hurled it in his direction. The impact struck him on the shoulder, momentarily disorienting him. It was a fleeting victory, for the Tall Man remained undeterred, his expression morphing into a twisted smile that sent shivers down my spine.

He lunged at me, his knife gleaming malevolently in the dim light. Instinctively, I dodged his attack, my resolve solidifying. Spotting a briefcase on a nearby desk, I snatched it up, wielding it as a makeshift weapon. Blow after blow rained down upon the Tall Man, my determination propelling me forward. Finally, his grip on the knife faltered, and it clattered to the ground, freeing me momentarily from his lethal threat.

But the moment of respite was short-lived. Without warning, a figure clad in a yellow hazmat suit leaped upon me from behind, ensnaring me in a bear hug. The air was crushed from my lungs, and I heard a voice exclaim triumphantly that they had captured me. Before I could comprehend the situation, a rope tied around the figure's body whisked us away, its unseen force propelling us through the darkness.

My senses reeled as we materialized in a dimly lit room, filled with an array of cameras and monitors. Figures surrounded us, engrossed in their activities, jotting notes on charts and operating cameras. Amidst the chaos, someone shouted for Smith to take hold of me. The man in the yellow hazmat suit lunged toward me once again, but his movements were impeded by the rope attached to him, held back by some intricate pulley system. Determined, Smith began to untie himself, his eyes fixed on me with malicious intent.

However, before he could close the distance, a door swung open, and a sliver of light from the outside world pierced through the darkness. In an instant, I sprung to my feet, clutching the briefcase tightly. Without a second thought, I sprinted toward the door, propelled by a surge of adrenaline. Confusion washed over the security guards who stood in my path, their hesitation evident as they debated whether to shoot or restrain me.

With every ounce of strength and determination, I burst through the threshold, stepping into the long-awaited freedom of the outside world. The air filled my lungs, and the warmth of the sun bathed my face, a stark contrast to the lifeless confines I had endured for so long. Driven by an instinctual need to escape, I continued running

Mostly Better Now

I ran several blocks before I was able to jump on a bus, I made my way to the other side of the side city all the while twisting my neck around to see I was going to be chased down by who knows what, but there was nothing, just the usual sounds of a busy city.

I jumped off the bus and continued running for several blocks, my eyes darting around, half-expecting some man in a yellow hazmat suit to jump out from every alleyway. However, the bustling sounds of the city were the only accompaniment to my frantic footsteps. There were no signs of pursuit, no eerie presence lingering in the shadows. It seemed that I had finally shaken off the horrors of the Backrooms.

Seeking safety and some form of refuge, I made my way to a nearby hospital. In a city like New York, a missing ear and finger were unlikely to raise many eyebrows. The medical staff didn't question the circumstances behind my injuries; any fabricated story would suffice. They swiftly attended to my wounds, administering necessary shots and skillfully stitching up my ear. While I had sadly lost my finger, the rest of my fingers were spared.

My arm was infused with fluids, replenishing my dehydrated body, and powerful pain medication was administered to alleviate the discomfort. Exhaustion washed over me, and I slipped into a deep, dreamless sleep for two uninterrupted days. It was a welcome respite from the harrowing experiences that had plagued me.

As my time at the hospital drew to a close, I was preparing to leave when a nurse rushed toward me, a sense of urgency in her eyes. She reminded me not to forget my briefcase, a revelation that jolted me back to reality. I had completely forgotten about the briefcase I had grabbed during the intense encounter with the Tall Man. The nurse said I looked handsome with a briefcase, I smiled, and then my tooth popped out, I told you I was "mostly" better.

Excitement coursed through my veins as I gingerly took hold of the heavy briefcase, brimming with unknown contents. I couldn't contain my curiosity, my mind whirling with possibilities. The nurse commented that I looked rather dashing with a briefcase, eliciting a smile from me. Just as I thought my ordeal was finally over, a sudden jolt of surprise caused my tooth to pop out unexpectedly. It was a gentle reminder that while I had emerged from the Backrooms, I was still nursing the scars of my traumatic journey.

With a mix of relief and lingering trepidation, I stepped out of the hospital, clutching the briefcase tightly, uncertain of what lay ahead. The road to recovery was just beginning, both physically and emotionally. Yet, armed with newfound resilience and a reminder of the strength I had summoned within the depths of the Backrooms, I was determined to forge a new path, one that would lead me away from the haunting memories of that surreal realm.

Recovery

I trudged wearily back to my apartment, a sense of exhaustion and weariness still clinging to me. As I approached my mailbox, a stack of past due bills peeked out, a reminder of the mundane responsibilities that awaited me. However, I had little interest in dealing with them at the moment. I simply walked past, brushing off the mundane concerns, much like I had brushed off the strange figures monitoring my apartment from outside.

Rhonda: When you get a chance head over to my apartment, don't go in but see if there is a white utility van still sitting across the street. I don't know who they are, but they were keeping an eye on me until I slipped out my window two nights ago. I was planning on resting and taking my time for a few weeks, but another tooth popped out. I'm also losing some hair; I find clumps of it all over my apartment. I needed some answers fast.

The Briefcase

I carefully examined the contents of the briefcase, my curiosity piqued by the assortment of items within. As I spilled them onto the floor, three books caught my attention: an architecture book, a physics book, and a biology book. Initially, I couldn't discern what connection these subjects had, but it became clear as I delved into the accompanying notebook.

The notebook was a compilation of writings, partly in English and partly in German. I realized that it held valuable information, although deciphering the German portions would require the aid of Google Translate. I made a mental note to dedicate a night to the task, eager to uncover any hidden insights.

Among the notebook's pages, I stumbled upon a family picture, accompanied by an address. The address led to a place called Beach Haven, a location that suggested it might be a family vacation house. Intrigued, I pondered the significance of this discovery. If families typically did not sell their vacation homes, it raised the possibility that someone associated with the property might possess valuable information or be able to shed light on the enigmatic figure mentioned in the briefcase—Dr. Z%#$%.

The name, although obscured, presented a tantalizing lead. Who was Dr. Z%#$%? What role did they play in the events we had experienced in the Backrooms? I realized that unraveling this mystery might hold the key to understanding the strange occurrences and finding a sense of closure.

With a mix of anticipation and trepidation, I resolved to embark on a journey to Beach Haven. There, I hoped to uncover more about the vacation house, its history, and the potential ties it held to the enigmatic Dr. Z%#$%. The prospect of finding answers buoyed my spirits, even as uncertainty and the weight of our shared experiences continued to gnaw at the edges of my consciousness.

I knew that the road ahead would be filled with more questions than answers, but armed with the newfound knowledge from the briefcase, I felt a renewed sense of purpose.

As I closed the briefcase, I couldn't help but feel a mixture of excitement and apprehension. The journey to Beach Haven held the promise of uncovering hidden truths, but it also carried the weight of the unknown. With determination in my heart, I prepared to embark on the next leg of our quest, ready to confront the secrets that awaited me in the coastal town of Beach Haven.

Alex Z%#$%

It was well past midnight when I mustered the courage to knock on the door of the Beach Haven address. Impatience had gotten the better of me, and the need for answers propelled me forward, overriding any concerns about the late hour.

A young girl answered the door, her inquisitive eyes studying me intently. I introduced myself and explained that I believed I possessed her grandfather's briefcase. As I mentioned Dr. Z%#$%, her reaction was immediate—a mixture of surprise and intrigue. She opened the door wider, inviting me inside.

I couldn't help but notice the peculiar coincidence—Alex, as she introduced herself, had two fingers missing, mirroring my own disfigurement. It was an uncanny connection, as if the Backrooms had left its mark on both of us in similar ways.

We spent the remainder of the night sharing our stories, each revealing our harrowing experiences within the enigmatic depths of the Backrooms. As we delved deeper into our narratives, a sense of camaraderie formed between us—a bond forged in the crucible of shared adversity. However, there was something about Alex that piqued my curiosity—a subtle air of mystery that lingered beneath her words.

Amidst the exchange of tales, Alex seemed to possess a profound knowledge of the Backrooms—a familiarity that extended beyond her own journey. She hinted at an understanding of the specific part of the Backrooms I had traversed, suggesting she had encountered similar environments or levels. It was an intriguing revelation—one that stirred a mixture of curiosity and caution within me.

Though Alex appeared forthcoming and genuine, there was a subtle hesitation in her voice at times, a fleeting flicker in her eyes that suggested she might be withholding certain details. It was as if she carried a secret, a hidden piece of the puzzle that she wasn't quite ready to reveal.

As we discussed our respective paths, I couldn't help but wonder what else lay beneath the surface of Alex's experiences. Was there more to her story than met the eye? What could she be concealing? It was a thought that lingered in the back of my mind, adding a layer of intrigue to our newfound alliance.

Our conversation concluded with an agreement to join forces—an alliance born out of mutual determination to unravel the mysteries of the Backrooms. With our combined knowledge and shared resilience, we hoped to navigate the treacherous depths of the enigmatic realm, inching closer to the truth that lay hidden within.

Alex then broke the bad news.

Three months to live

Rhonda: I hope you are sitting down. I don't know how else to tell you, but Alex told me I only have three months to live. I sat in disbelief, clutching the letter in my trembling hands. Three months. That was the time I had left to find the cure and save my own life. The gravity of the situation hit me like a ton of bricks, and fear crept into every corner of my being. How could this be happening? How could a mere encounter with a water fountain lead to such a dire prognosis?

My mind raced, trying to comprehend the enormity of the situation. The Vampire water fountain, once an innocuous feature of the Backrooms, had now become my nemesis, infecting me with a malevolent force that threatened to consume my very existence. It felt like a cruel twist of fate, a macabre game where the stakes were nothing short of life and death.

The words "teeth and hair falling out" echoed in my mind, a haunting reminder of the visible signs of my impending decline. I touched my own hair, feeling a mix of panic and sadness as strands slipped through my fingers. My reflection in the mirror revealed a face that was rapidly losing its vitality, teeth gradually giving way to emptiness. It was a nightmare come to life.

Yet, amid the despair, a flicker of hope ignited within me. Alex, the enigmatic individual who seemed to hold the key to my survival, knew the location of the cure. But it was a place I had hoped never to return to—the Backrooms, a labyrinthine realm that had already brought me so much anguish and fear. However, desperate times called for desperate measures, and I had no choice but to face the dreaded levels once more.

I reached out to Alex, seeking guidance and reassurance. We met in a clandestine location, hidden away from prying eyes. The sight of Alex, shrouded in an air of mystery, made me wonder what secrets they held. Were they truly an ally, or did they harbor their own hidden motives?

Alex spoke with a calmness that belied the urgency of our situation. They explained that we would need to delve into the depths of the Backrooms, navigating through its twisted corridors and treacherous levels to reach the lab on level 7. It would be a perilous journey, fraught with unseen dangers and unknown adversaries.

The path ahead was uncertain, but I had no choice but to trust Alex. We pored over the books and notebook from my grandfather's briefcase, searching for any clues that could lead us to the lab and its life-saving remedy. The mixture of English and German in the notebook added to the enigma, requiring us to decipher its cryptic messages and unravel its secrets.

Going Back

Alex and I have made the difficult decision to venture back into the treacherous depths of the Backrooms in search of the cure that could save my life. The urgency of our mission is further intensified by the rapid deterioration of my health. Each passing day brings more losses—teeth and hair, the visible markers of my diminishing vitality.

Alex's entry point into the Backrooms has been sealed off, leaving mine as the only viable pathway. Last night, we carefully inspected and confirmed that my entry point remains open. It is through this portal that we will once again step into the nightmarish realm that has haunted my existence.

Our plan is to travel through the levels, ascending towards level 7 where the lab is rumored to be located. We anticipate that the journey will be long and arduous, possibly taking a month or even longer. Time is no longer a luxury I possess, and I can only hope that my body can endure the trials that lie ahead.

I must admit, Rhonda, that despite our shared goal, there is something about Alex that unsettles me. There are moments when her demeanor seems shrouded in secrecy, as if she is hiding something. I cannot shake the feeling that there is more to her than meets the eye. Nevertheless, I must put my trust in her expertise and knowledge of the Backrooms, for she has spent years navigating its labyrinthine corridors in search of her own answers.

Alex will be sending you her notes soon, which I hope will shed light on the intricacies of our mission and provide you with a deeper understanding of the enigmatic realm we are venturing into. I apologize for my inability to fully explain the intricacies of our journey, as words fail to capture the true essence of the Backrooms and its mysteries.

As I write this, we stand on the precipice of uncertainty, filled with equal measures of hope and trepidation. We have packed our belongings and made the necessary preparations for the challenging journey that lies ahead. The unknown awaits us, and we are ready to confront it head-on.

I ask for your prayers and well wishes, Rhonda. They will be our guiding light amidst the darkness that surrounds us. Please know that your support means the world to me, and I am grateful for your unwavering presence throughout this harrowing ordeal. We are packed and ready to go. Wish us luck. Please pray for us.

-Ollie

Backrooms: Beginnings

Dr Z

Ever since I could recall, I've been aware of a chasm of difference separating me from the ordinary. My recollections were nebulous, like wisps of foggy memories that seem borrowed rather than mine. I was aware of my uniqueness, yet harbored an inner belief that there were others like me, tethered to the same spectral abyss— the Backrooms, a grim realm of suffering and expiration. The Backrooms subsist on our essence, bending our sanity to its will and blurring the lines between morality and sin.

This narrative is my recollection of a project - a sinister enterprise that bore the Backrooms into existence and the experimental atrocities we conducted there. They called me Dr Z - a moniker they ascribed to me when I enlisted for this venture. The military machine has always been ravenous for science, its appetite unfettered in the pursuit of devastating armaments. My project, however, had nothing to do with explosives, and yet ironically, it has been responsible for the extermination of an unquantifiable number of lives, far surpassing the tally of any bomb they could have ever engineered.

I was merely performing my duty, or so I told myself. However, somewhere in the silent chambers of my conscience, I knew I was the puppeteer behind the macabre show. I cloaked myself in the lie that the fatalities were not on my hands, that they were mere figments of an unreal world. But the truth, raw and ugly, remained, eating at the edges of my denial. I was just doing my job, but I knew deep down that I was responsible for it all. I lied to myself that the deaths were not my fault, none of them were real.

Interview

The undertaking I was handpicked for bore the cryptic code name, R22. The origins of R22 traced back to the conclusion of the Second World War, shrouded in mystery and intrigue. It represented a peculiar radio frequency, one that theoretically did not exist, not beyond the secure walls of government institutions, at least. The ownership rights to this esoteric frequency were held by the enigmatic organization known as Blacktree. Usually, the nature of a project became apparent to me after a handful of interviews, but R22 had successfully baffled me.

At the helm of the interview panel was a man designated as Dr C. Two other scientists, their faces etched with stern expressions, flanked him. They embarked on an inquisition of my knowledge for what felt like an eternity, scrutinizing my expertise. When they were eventually satisfied that my credentials weren't mere hyperbole, they wordlessly rose from their seats and departed, leaving me alone in the cold scrutiny of Dr C.

Dr C held me in his hawk-like gaze for several uneasy moments. The silence in the room was oppressive, punctuated only by the soft hum of the ventilation system. Then, quite unexpectedly, he rolled his eyes,

and laughed like a lunatic. The laugh was devoid of warmth, sounding more like the unhinged amusement of a madman, the sort of laugh that sent a chill down your spine. It was a sound that lingered in the air long after it had ceased, leaving an indelible imprint on the ambience of the room.

Dr C

With the echo of his disturbing laughter still hanging in the air, Dr C finally broke his silence. "The only qualifications needed for this project are a rudimentary comprehension of science, peppered with a dash of madness. I've already interviewed people far superior in terms of experience and intelligence, but they couldn't make it far," he said with an uncanny glint in his eyes.

"I am Dr C, and should you choose to embark on this project, you shall be christened Dr Z. I'm running out of letters to assign to doctors, so I fear you might be the last," he said with an insidious smirk that chilled me to the bone.

He slid an envelope across the table. It held an address and a standard top-secret non-disclosure agreement, sternly stating that should I dare to divulge any information, government operatives armed to the teeth would be dispatched to pay me a visit. "If the offer appeals to you, be at this location tomorrow," he declared, his voice as cold as ice.

Taking the envelope, I shook his hand, assuring him of my presence the following day. As I left, a peculiar feeling gnawed at me. I had the unsettling impression that should anything go awry in the lab, Dr C would be the first to abandon ship, probably wearing that maniacal grin and echoing his haunting laugh. I hypothesized that his inherent madness was perhaps the secret to his survival in this unchartered territory.

The BackOffices

The morning alarm rang ominously early as I prepared for the trials of New York City's notorious downtown traffic. The project's lucrative remuneration, promising to double my previous year's earnings, took the edge off the early start and the taxing commute. The destination was an antiquated office edifice situated in the heart of the city.

Upon entering the building, I scanned the directory panel flanking the elevators, but the office number was conspicuously absent. Perplexed, I turned to the receptionist for guidance, and she nonchalantly directed me towards the building's rear.

An imposing security gateway marked the entry to a secluded area referred to as the BackOffices. This discreet section was dedicated to clandestine government projects and was armed to the teeth with an impressive array of military apparatus, a testament to its strategic importance.

Once admitted into the BackOffices, I was ushered further into the famed Backrooms, a labyrinthine expanse nested within the BackOffices. A sense of foreboding washed over me, as I questioned the implications of my choices.

In the research center, an eerie silence was punctuated by the faint hum of technology and muffled voices emanating from behind closed doors. Strangely, despite the myriad rooms and audible signs of activity, there wasn't a single soul in sight. The hallway, dimly lit and pulsating with unseen energy, was a complex web of electrical wires, snaking up and down the walls like vital veins and arteries, supplying life to the heart of the BackOffices.

17

Upon reaching the terminus of the hallway, I knocked on a sturdy wooden door, flanked by a metallic plaque inscribed with 'BackRooms Project R22.' After a brief wait, I tested the door, and to my surprise, it swung open after the second attempt with the knob.

Inside the room, Dr C sat at a table, his penetrating gaze fixed on me. Before I could utter a greeting, he held up a finger to his lips and gestured for silence, the universal 'shush' sign borrowed from librarians worldwide. He passed me a note. The instructions written on it were peculiar: keep silent, walk ten feet to an antique phone booth, listen to the receiver for a minute, then sit down across from him without uttering a word for five minutes.

Following the instructions, I made my way to the phone booth and picked up the receiver. Dr C's measured voice filled my ears, "Good morning! Welcome to Project R22. I hope we have a great first day." I initially assumed it was a pre-recorded message until I heard my own voice echoing from the receiver a few seconds later, saying "seventeen."

I shot a perplexed glance at Dr C, but his lips hadn't moved since I entered the room. He gestured for me to hang up the receiver and join him at the table. We sat there, in a mutual silence, his unusual grin a stark contrast against his pale complexion.

After five minutes of disconcerting silence, he produced a microphone and a frayed hat brimming with folded papers. He motioned for me to pick one. As I reached into the hat, he spoke into the microphone, "Good morning! Welcome to Project R22. I hope we have a great first day." He then encouraged me to read the selected paper out loud.

Upon unfolding the slip, I discovered the number '17' inscribed on it. Mirroring the note, I repeated "seventeen" into the microphone. With that, Dr C unplugged the device and erupted into that eerily familiar laughter, underscoring the role of insanity in this unprecedented project.

5 Minutes

Dr C's fit of laughter subsided as he noticed my befuddled expression. His mirth was replaced by a serious demeanor, and he proceeded to delve into an intricate physics lecture that lasted an hour.

The gist of his explanation was that R22 emerged from the ambitious pursuits of scientists at Blacktree. These researchers sought to manipulate radio waves to induce proton infusion into uranium. The more unstable, the better, was their audacious motto. To this end, they experimented with radio waves, trying to create a form of force field around a room. They tried both short and long wave variants, but to no avail. Then, suddenly... that was it. No one truly knows how the discovery occurred, but it swiftly led to a government-backed patent the very next day.

Despite millions of dollars funneled into the project, Blacktree couldn't ascertain its practical applications. Dr C revealed that the room we were in was encased by four R22 machines, capable of transmitting a message five minutes into the past. His explanation was punctuated by more peals of laughter.

Our task, he clarified, was to find a worthwhile application for this temporal communication to justify the project's considerable expense. Profit, after all, was the lifeblood of the company, and time was running out, in more ways than one.

"If you can't find a practical application for this five-minute time-traveling phone call, Dr Z, then this project is doomed," he stated with a gravity that underlined the enormity of my assignment. The last scientist in a long line of predecessors, the fate of Project R22 rested on my shoulders.

Time Travel

I was reeling from the revelation. Time travel, a concept I had only dissected within the confines of scientific theories, was materializing before my eyes. The enormity of it left me dazed and astounded as I grappled with the reality at the end of the day.

How on earth could we possibly commercialize this? How could we make five-minute time-traveling phone calls, spanning just ten feet, appeal to a profit-hungry shareholder? The technology was groundbreaking, awe-inspiring even, but would it merely bore the stakeholders who held the project's fate in their hands? I wrestled with these questions on my journey home, shaking my head in disbelief at the thought of having witnessed time travel.

Upon reaching home, I instinctively lifted the phone receiver, half expecting to hear my own voice from five minutes ago. Instead, all I heard was the droning of the dial tone. It seemed my reality was confined to the BackOffices.

I decided to tweak my personal 'insanity knob' up a notch, readying myself for the wild ride I had unwittingly signed up for. As I turned in for the night, I silently reaffirmed to myself to just roll with it. This was my new reality, as bewildering as it was.

Profits

Inventing time travel was one thing, profiting from it was an entirely different beast. I pondered how we could capitalize on hearing a voice five minutes into the future from just ten feet away. It felt paradoxical—possessing such a groundbreaking tool, yet it seemed somewhat redundant.

I contemplated running a gambling scheme based on sports results, something I was quite familiar with due to my past run-ins with betting (one of the reasons I'd accepted this unusual job). Unfortunately, the timing of closing bets at baseball games or horse races couldn't be manipulated with just a five-minute window into the future.

The only viable profit-generating idea I could conceive involved transforming our operations into a futuristic fortune-telling venture. We had the fittingly eerie ambiance of the Backrooms in the BackOffices. All we needed was a crystal ball. However, Dr C wasn't taken by the idea. I suspected he'd already watched several predecessors wrestle with these same frustrations, racking their brains for profitable applications of our technology.

Despite being incredibly intelligent, Dr C didn't often suggest original ideas. His main claim to originality was an odd ritual he conducted every Tuesday. To demonstrate his 'intelligence', he'd invite a group of other scientists from the BackOffices and attempt to answer five questions that they would pose.

The setup was always the same. At precisely 11:55 am, Dr C would carry a stack of books into the phone booth and pick up the receiver. He'd wait until his voice echoed from the future, reciting the five questions the scientists were about to ask him. We would then scour the books for the answers to these questions. Once we had the answers ready, there'd be a knock at the door. The scientists would enter, handing Dr C a piece of paper with the five questions. He'd read the questions aloud, using a microphone hidden under the table, and promptly answer them as though he'd known in advance what they were going to ask. After the baffled scientists left the room, he'd bask in the pleasure of his trick, his boisterous laughter filling the room. This charade satisfied him for about an hour before we returned to the brain-racking task of finding a way to monetize time travel.

Paradox

I began to experiment with the paradox that had been gnawing at me. I would step into the phone booth, lift the receiver, and listen to my own voice relay a message. Five minutes later, I'd repeat the same message into the microphone. On occasion, I'd try altering the message, but it never changed what I had initially heard. Even if I decided to remain silent, the memory of what I had heard on the receiver five minutes prior remained intact. It was as if I were investigating whether the future had a distinct, unchangeable path, or if it was pliable.

On the subsequent Tuesday, I resolved to test one last theory. At 11:55 am, Dr C and I picked up the receiver and listened to the five questions, diligently noting the answers. The familiar knock on the door at 12:00 pm signaled the entrance of the scientists. In a swift move, I dashed to the door and discreetly handed the lead scientist a separate list of five questions I'd devised that morning. With a wink, I whispered, "Trust me, this will stump him."

Perusing the new questions, the lead scientist cracked a smile and handed the revised list to Dr C. I swiftly pocketed the original list. Dr C proceeded to read out the questions and provided the correct answers, much to everyone's astonishment. The lead scientist, visibly stunned, knocked over his chair as he shot up, casting me a glance before hurriedly leaving the room, once again bested.

When I asked Dr C how he knew all the answers, he simply replied that those were the ones he had heard on the receiver five minutes ago. I pulled out the original list of questions, which were entirely different from the ones I had given him. Something had indeed changed. Had I altered the future? Or was it the past that I had modified? But how? What was different this time? I sensed I was on the brink of a significant breakthrough.

New Approach

Further testing led to an array of theories, but we eventually converged on one: We surmised that we were unable to alter the timeline within the R22 bubble. The event with the altered questions only occurred because the interaction with the passing of the new list of questions to the lead scientist had taken place outside the bubble. This realization sparked an innovative idea in me.

Instead of pointing the R22 machines at each other to create a circular bubble, we repositioned them in a straight line to construct a wall of R22 energy. Standing outside this newly shaped bubble, we unleashed the R22 waves straight into the BackRooms office.

With this configuration, it felt like we had reoriented the structure of time itself, opening the possibility to manipulate events on the other side of the wall, within the BackRooms. This breakthrough marked a significant shift in our understanding of the project, offering the potential to influence events outside our immediate space.

Still, this did not completely address the objective of monetizing the technology. We now had a tool that allowed for interaction across the time-space boundary, but we still struggled to find a way to apply this concept in a profitable manner. Nevertheless, this was progress. We had taken a significant stride towards understanding and manipulating the fabric of time itself, something no other scientist could claim. We were exploring new frontiers, rewriting the rules of reality as we knew it.

Going In

Dr C and I were standing outside of the office looking at the row of R22 machine blasting the energy waves into the Backrooms office. Not knowing what was happening in the Backrooms with the new configuration of the R22 waves I put on a makeshift yellow safety suit; Dr C tied a rope around me just in case he needed to pull me out. The door to the office felt heavier and harder to pull open, I had to use two hands just to make it budge. I took a few steps in, I had to push my body inside, it felt as if I was walking into a head wind. Once inside of the room I felt a jerk, it felt just like when a train started to move and everyone shuffles around to grab something to hold on to. With the new configuration we decided to start off with a simple test. I walked over to the receiver and listen to a message I was going to say in five minutes, it was the same message on a piece of paper in my hand. Everything matched up as we expected, I made my way back over to the door, but it was stuck. I pushed and pushed but it didn't budge, the closer to the door I got it felt as if the R22 waves were pushing me back even more.

I finally had to give up, catch my breath, and go back to the middle of the room. I felt queasy and threw up in my suit. I tried to be careful when I removed my helmet, but still my lunch got all over my hair and it ran down my shirt. Once I gathered myself, I tugged on the rope that was attached to my waist. The rope led under the door to the safety of Dr C. I tugged and tugged but nothing.

After an hour everything seemed to settle down, my body adjusted to the force I first experience and I was now freely able to move around except for opening the door, that still appeared to be stuck. I looked at my watch and three hours had already gone by. I can only imagine that something went wrong on the outside and Dr C had to run over to the other scientists for help opening the door.

A few more hours went by, I yelled and kicked at the door. Still nothing, no help from the outside.

Copy

Suddenly, an unseen force yanked me towards the back of the room. At first, I assumed my vision was playing tricks on me as I saw two of everything, but it wasn't double vision – it was the room duplicating itself. Every single object was replicated, including me. I watched in shock as the duplicate room was tugged away, my doppelgänger included. Our eyes met, and we stood in stunned silence. My duplicate glanced down at his hands, then around the room, like a newborn taking in his surroundings. "Are you the copy or am I?" he asked. His question sparked a flood of my own. I barely had time to answer before I saw his body pressed against the back wall, an invisible force pulling him away.

In my peripheral vision, a pair of spectral hands emerged from the wall, grasping my duplicate. The hands belonged to yet another version of myself, this one aged, with long hair and a beard. He bore a large cut across his face and a missing set of teeth. How long had he been there? Where had he come from?

We stared at each other, three versions of the same man, each from a different time. Then, the older copy lunged at me, knocking me off my feet. He brandished a crude weapon, no doubt fashioned from office furniture. Just as he was about to strike, my other duplicate intervened, and the room jerked violently once more.

The force pinned both duplicates against the back wall as the room duplicated itself again. In the struggle, the copies were pulled through the wall, disappearing from my view. The sound of their struggle continued from the other side, ending with the triumphant yell of the older copy.

The room started to pull me again. I tugged at the rope tied around my waist, the lifeline that tethered me to the real world. I watched as the blood-soaked hands of the older copy tried to claw their way back through the wall, still clutching the bloodied club. I felt a sharp pull at my waist, jerking me towards the door. I looked over my shoulder to see Dr. C pulling me out.

Once I was safely outside, I shut the machines down. Dr C nonchalantly commented that my five minutes were up. I insisted I'd spent ten hours inside the room, but my watch had stopped, and looking out the window, the sun was still high in the sky. Trembling, I opened the door to peek inside. There was no sign of my older duplicate. Somehow, I had spent an entire workday in what was, to the outside world, only five minutes.

Murder

Once my nerves settled, the grim reality of what had transpired hit me. Had I witnessed my own murder? And how could I report such an incident? Explaining to the authorities that I saw myself kill another version of me would only land me in a mental institution.

Sharing my experiences with Dr. C, I realized how absurd my story must sound. Responding to my account, Dr. C handed me a folder from his filing cabinet. Inside was my signed 'Top Secret Research' contract – an agreement to work on this clandestine project. Sandwiched between a page with my signature and countless pages of legal jargon were explicit clauses: any breach of this contract could result in life imprisonment.

There was no call to the police that night. No calls on any subsequent nights when I saw the horrors that lurked in the Backrooms. A feeling of helplessness washed over me. I felt trapped, cornered. My stomach churned with anxiety.

Sensing my discomfort, Dr. C put his hand on my shoulder, offering a small envelope. "This should make things more tolerable," he said. Inside the envelope was a check – an entire year's salary. He assured me that more would follow if I continued my work and stayed silent.

Dr. C stepped closer, his scent invading my space. "Don't ever let me catch you spilling any information about our work," he warned, his voice barely more than a whisper. "The police will be the least of your worries. The company will bury you so deep, you'll never see the light of day again."

Suddenly, the extent of my situation was made brutally clear: I was in a game that I could only play, not quit. But the stakes of this game were much higher than I had ever realized. With the threat of this new reality hanging over me, I had to make a choice. To keep silent and continue down this path, or risk everything to expose the truth. The haunting memories of the Backrooms weighed heavily on my conscience. But for now, I had to decide how to survive, not just for me, but for every version of me out there.

Not The First Time

I was about to leave for the day when a question nagged at me. I looked at Dr. C, who was engrossed in his documents, and asked, "Is this the first time I have been part of this experiment?"

He glanced up at me, his eyes calm but calculating. "No," he said simply. "You have been part of experiments in the Backrooms before. But this is the first time you remember it."

His revelation made my blood run cold. According to him, I had been part of these strange, twisted experiments for a month. Given the time disparity inside the Backrooms, he estimated that I had spent approximately a year inside, with thousands of copies of myself being created and destroyed in a loop of time I had no recollection of.

His next words were even more chilling. He explained that this was the first instance where a copy of myself had made it out from the back wall, which prompted him to intervene. "We need to be cautious," he said, "We can't predict what might happen if a duplicate manages to escape. Though," he added with a sardonic grin, "it would be fascinating to find out, wouldn't it?"

His laughter echoed in the room, a stark contrast to the heaviness that had settled in my chest. He scribbled a few more notes before glancing up at me. "Take a month off," he commanded. "We'll be bringing in new people, and the Backrooms need some reconfiguration for the upcoming experiments."

As I exited the facility, his words resonated in my mind. I felt like a lab rat caught in a relentless cycle of terrifying experiments, while my countless copies met unknown fates within the confines of the Backrooms. The depth of what I was entangled in was now clearer than ever, and I was left grappling with this chilling new reality.

Welcome Back

The scene that greeted me after my month-long hiatus was drastically different from what I remembered. The facility was now heavily guarded, with stern-faced individuals positioned at the building entrance and office door. Their uniform gave no indication of their affiliation - military or otherwise, and they remained taciturn, responding only to my awkward nods with curt nods of their own as they let me pass.

My office, once a small and cramped space, had been thoroughly transformed. The majority of the walls had been knocked down, and even the ceiling had been raised, effectively expanding our workspace to occupy most of the floor. Four R22 machines were positioned around the periphery, their formidable presence dwarfing the encapsulated Backrooms. The previously cohabited projects were either canceled or relocated, with the exclusive focus now on our time experiment.

The Wednesday trivia scientists had been integrated into our team, their expertise now contributing to our endeavors. Desks across the new expanse of the office were littered with notes, diagrams, and brainstorming ideas. The remarkable discoveries from the past experiments had sparked a torrent of potential directions for our research, each one more audacious than the last.

Dr C approached me, his face revealing a mix of concern and anticipation. He asked how I was and whether I was ready to dive back into work. I responded affirmatively, my curiosity overpowering any residual apprehension. He went on to inform me that all new team members had undergone the same experiment I had before joining. This shared experience, he explained, was crucial to ensure everyone had a deep, personal understanding of the complexities and mysteries of the Backrooms. But it also came with a caveat: What was learned in the office, stayed in the office. Our collective understanding was a secret to be safeguarded, never to be shared outside the confines of these walls.

New Backrooms

Dr. C led me towards the revamped Backrooms. In addition to the original room, they had created an opening in the back wall, which acted as a gateway to the multitude of duplicated rooms produced during each experiment. The room had been furnished to resemble an ordinary office space, complete with desks, chairs, filing cabinets, and decorative items. The illusion was only broken by the presence of a newly constructed viewing area, adjoined to the side of the main room.

This viewing area, encased in thick, reinforced glass, had its separate entrance, facilitating unrestricted movement for the scientists during the experiments. It was designed to be outside the area of effect of the R22 machines, thereby preventing any unwanted duplication of the personnel or equipment in the viewing room. It was an ingenious addition to the setup, providing us a safe zone from where we could observe and analyze the phenomena in the main room without being directly impacted by it.

A sense of relief washed over me as I realized the implications of the viewing room. With this new setup, I could conduct and observe the experiments without the risk of having another doppelgänger of myself emerging from the back wall. The thought of repeating the earlier ordeal was still fresh in my mind and left a sour taste. This new arrangement was indeed a welcome development.

Pigs

The following day, a truck arrived. Its cargo was quite vocal - our next test subject was an enthusiastic pig. Once the pig was settled into the main room, we retreated to the safety and comfort of the viewing area. Our anticipation was palpable as we powered up the R22 machines and watched the spectacle unfold.

Just as anticipated, the room and everything in it, including the pig, were duplicated. The copy of the pig trotted through the newly created opening in the back wall, sniffed at the original, and then went on exploring the room alongside its new 'friend'.

As the experiment proceeded and hundreds of pigs were duplicated, a pattern started to emerge. The older duplicates seemed to slowly fade out, their distinct features blurring until they resembled ghostly apparitions. And in a matter of a few seconds, they vanished altogether, as if they had never existed.

By the end of the day, the room was a testament to the mind-bending experiments we had been conducting. The overpowering scent of hundreds of pigs lingered in the air, a sensory reminder of the artificial lives that had briefly thrived in the room.

Back in our lab, we donned our metaphorical philosopher's hats to analyze the day's proceedings. We pondered on existential questions and debated on the ethical implications of our work. Were we playing God, creating life just to watch it fade away? Or were we pioneers, pushing the boundaries of scientific understanding?

Each scientist penned down their observations and musings. Dr C gathered the reports, meticulously filing them away. Another day of groundbreaking research had come to a close. The journey, though fraught with ethical and existential dilemmas, was far from over.

Dead Pigs

The following day brought a new twist to our experiment. A medical doctor, armed with a bag full of syringes, came to join us. We settled the pig in the main room, anxiously awaiting the inevitable replication. Once the duplicated pig made its appearance, the doctor swiftly administered an injection. Immediately after the injection, he began timing the pig's reaction with a stopwatch.

The experiment soon took a grim turn. Every injected duplicate succumbed within a matter of minutes, each one displaying different distressing symptoms. Convulsions, bloody coughs, sudden internal bleeding, irrational frenzies... all these horrific scenarios played out in front of us over the next few weeks as we continuously ran the experiment with different syringes.

As the days wore on, I found it increasingly challenging to reconcile with the gruesome sight of dying pigs. A numbing sense of disconnection pervaded my thoughts. What was my role in all this? How did my work morph from an exploration of physics to overseeing a morbid spectacle?

Then, a minor incident led to a significant breakthrough. One day, a doctor accidentally left his stopwatch in the room during a replication cycle. Upon retrieving it, he discovered that the duplicated stopwatch had stopped functioning. This led us to speculate that the force exerted during the duplication process might have stretched and damaged the mainspring of the copied watch, rendering it inoperative.

This seemingly insignificant observation had profound implications for our experiments. We could now use a watch to differentiate between the original and duplicate subjects. By attaching a watch to the collar of the original pig, we could ensure the correct pig was being injected by checking whether the watch was functioning.

This was a great discovery since we sometimes couldn't tell between the original pig and the copies. The doctor would now clip on a watch to the original pigs' collar before they entered the Backrooms. Right before each injection they would now check the watch to make sure they were injecting the correct pig.

This simple discover would now bring the experiments to a whole new level.

Smiths

The following week, I returned to an entirely different scene in the office. The stench of pigs was gone, replaced by a single human subject. He was a young man in his twenties, clad in an Army uniform. The only identification on his attire was a name tag - "Smith." There were no indicators of his rank or division. Two watches clung to his wrist - a stark reminder of our new method of identification.

A glance at my fellow scientists confirmed my unease - every face in the room had taken on a grave, serious expression. We were on the brink of an endeavor far more daunting than anything we had undertaken before. The prospect of replicating a human, possibly resulting in his death, was chilling.

I attempted to leave, but Dr. C grabbed my shoulder, leading me to his desk. From a drawer, he produced an envelope - another bonus check. His words were eerily reassuring. "Just show up and sit in the viewing room. Keep your head down, read a book, hum to yourself - whatever it takes. You will get through this, just like the rest of us."

When the time came, we all entered the viewing room with an air of solemnity. The doctor blindfolded Smith and led him into the main room. We observed from the viewing area as the duplication process started. Once the copy was complete, the doctor returned to the room to verify Smith's identity via the functioning watch. He then led the original Smith out of the room and into the safety of the viewing area.

Returning to the bewildered duplicate, the doctor guided him to a chair and administered an injection. Within a minute, the duplicated Smith slumped over, lifeless. The disturbing procedure was repeated throughout the day, each iteration yielding the same grim result.

Small, Medium, and Large Smiths

The days blurred into a monotonous and grim pattern. Each dawn, a new Smith would emerge through the doors of our office. They were a diverse representation of humanity itself: from short to tall, slim to bulky, every variation of Smith made its appearance. But no matter the external variations, they all shared an identical silence, the same crisp Army uniform adorned with 'Smith' stitched in bold letters, and, most tragically, the same inescapable fate that awaited them: a death sentence within a minute of their birth.

These sessions, with their morbid underpinnings, felt like rehearsals for an even more sinister spectacle. My mind was in a constant state of unrest, wrestling with the shocking realities our experiments presented. There seemed to be no 'humane' way to die in the Backrooms. But amidst this grim reality, I sought and found cold solace in a singular truth: these beings were merely copies. They had no roots in the world, no family pining for their return, no past to reminisce about, and no future to anticipate.

To reconcile my moral qualms with the dystopian situation I found myself in, I convinced myself that these beings were devoid of the divine essence of life. They were artificial products of machinery, absent of the traditional process of conception and birth. No divine entity had breathed life into them. And the torment they showcased, could it really be called pain if they were devoid of a soul?

This became my daily ritual, a psychological lullaby I whispered to myself each morning and every night: They weren't real; they weren't human. They were mere replicas, soulless creations of a machine.

Let the Betting Begin

The experiment for the week was designed to measure the endurance of the Smith copy in the face of imminent death. The routine was simple: administer the injection and ask the Smith copy to read a book. The lethal cocktail took approximately fifteen minutes to work its sinister magic, during which Smith would attempt to get as far as possible through the text. Some days, Smith would manage to reach page six or seven before succumbing to the effects of the injection and collapsing dead.

In our attempts to acclimate to the reality of our work, we started to gamify the inevitable, placing bets on how many pages Smith could get through before his demise. Someone even suggested marking an 'X' on the floor, adding a new wager on whether Smith would land on the 'X' when his time came.

However, the dynamics of the experiment changed when the new set of injections caused the Smith copies to convulse violently before death. At times, they would hit the 'X', but the subsequent tremors would dislodge their bodies from the mark. To keep the game fair, we established a rule: for a bet to win, a dead Smith's body had to cover the 'X' for a full three seconds post-fall.

I never imagined that I could become so desensitized to witnessing death, let alone derive a form of morbid amusement from predicting its precise occurrence. But here I was, partaking in this grotesque spectacle, trying to ignore the screams of my conscience. Each time, I reminded myself: these weren't real people; they were merely copies.

Jesus Smith

They had to carry in the last Smith for this round because the Smith was already dead. As we sat there, uncertainty filling the room, I joked, "Five dollars says Smith comes back to life during the copy." It was meant as a light-hearted jest, but it hung in the air heavily. The notion that something or someone could come back to life within the Backrooms had never crossed our minds. Complex theories and ethical considerations filled our thoughts as the R22 machines hummed, initiating the copy process.

Once the duplication was complete, all eyes were drawn to the opening in the back wall. An eerie silence descended on the viewing room as we waited, the minutes stretching into an eternity. The stillness was shattered when, to our shock, the copied Smith emerged, alive and well.

The room remained silent as the doctor methodically recorded the event and moved to greet the resurrected Smith. The copy was guided to a chair and given the book to read. He began turning the pages, but his eyes frequently darted towards the corpse on the floor, the chilling mirror image of himself. The scientist administered the injection and, like clockwork, Smith collapsed dead after reaching page six. A shame he missed the 'X'—I could have won double that day.

Rinse and Repeat

Each week, the same Smiths returned, each earning a new epithet: Monday Smith, Tuesday Smith, Wednesday Smith, and so forth. The only exception was the 'Dead Smith' from our extraordinary experiment; he was conspicuously absent.

The first injection administered in this new series was fast-acting and seemed mercifully easy on the Smiths. The subsequent ones, however, were quite the opposite. The Backrooms became a theater of pain and suffering, each day revealing a new level of torment inflicted on the copies.

Every morning, I reiterated to myself: they were mere copies. And every night, before I drifted into troubled sleep, I repeated: they were mere copies. Still, despite these self-administered reassurances, I was a spectator to a macabre display of death in its countless, twisted forms. Eventually, the sheer horror and immorality of it all drove me to the edge—I could not bear to watch any longer.

The miraculous rebirth of the 'Dead Smith' the previous week, however, had rekindled my interest in the underlying principles of the Backrooms. I was driven by a newfound determination to understand how this extraordinary space functioned and, perhaps, uncover a means to mitigate the torment we were inflicting upon the Smiths.

Hiking

Our understanding and manipulation of the Backrooms had advanced. We could now control the rate at which the room replicated itself, from leisurely progression to a rapid flurry of hundreds of copies within a span of minutes. One day, I set the room to rapidly duplicate before slowing it down to a usual pace for the day's experiments. Equipped with a backpack carrying my lunch and some other supplies, I decided to venture through the extensive labyrinth of copied rooms before the day's testing began. A group of other scientists, also seeming wearied by the incessant screams and suffering, joined me.

As we ventured further from the original room, the relief was palpable. The distant, muffled echoes of Smith's tormented cries were easier to bear than the up-close reality. It took us about three hours to reach the end of the seemingly endless string of rooms. By the time we arrived, we noticed peculiar anomalies—the pictures on the walls had started to fade, and solid objects like desks and chairs were gradually losing their shape.

We were, in essence, explorers charting a new and unorthodox territory. The joy of discovery, of stepping away from the usual routine of torture and death, reinvigorated us. We felt a surge of excitement and a sense of purpose, the likes of which we hadn't felt in weeks. However, this respite was short-lived as we soon heard the familiar sounds of distress. Wednesday Smith came hurtling down the corridor, a chilling reminder of the dark reality we were attempting to escape from. He was screaming, with blood spewing from his mouth—an abrupt end to our brief moment of peace, and just another day in the Backrooms.

Biking

Our daily hikes were exhausting, and the return journey was particularly strenuous. To ease our travels, Dr C permitted us to bring in bicycles. Initially, the narrow passages made bike riding a challenge. We suffered a few bumps and crashes, but we persisted, adapting to the confined space. However, as we ventured further into the replication labyrinth, our accidents increased.

I initially attributed our clumsiness to fatigue, but soon noticed an odd curvature in the hallway. The further we travelled, the more apparent the bend became. After cycling several miles, I began to question whether the hallway was subtly spiraling, leading us in a circle.

We made occasional stops to observe the replicated rooms and record our findings. After the four hundredth copy, the pictures on the walls and other minor items had entirely disappeared. Upon reaching the five hundredth copy, the lights began to emit an irritating buzz and bathed the rooms in a sickly yellow light. The air felt stagnant, as if time itself had ceased to flow.

Continuing our journey, we noticed the hallway was now oscillating between left and right bends. We stopped at the six hundredth copy, the most distant one we'd reached so far. Here, all office furniture had vanished, and an unsettling swaying sensation permeated the hallway, as though we were on a ship on a choppy sea. We decided to turn back at this point, feeling nauseous—whether from the swaying or the surreal surroundings, we weren't sure. Despite this, the exploration had invigorated us, and we were eager to delve even deeper into the peculiar world of the Backrooms.

Motorcycling

I had become the unofficial motorcycle rider among us, able to maintain balance for more than a minute before colliding with the increasingly twisted walls. Others preferred the slower pace of bicycles, desiring any means to distance themselves from the harrowing screams echoing from the experimentation area. The new injections seemed to drive the Smith copies to such agony that I once saw Thursday Smith repeatedly bash his own head against the wall in a desperate attempt to alleviate the pain.

The scientists granted me a ten-minute head start on my motorcycle, as the exhaust quickly filled the rooms. Within minutes, I had passed the three hundredth room and pressed on to the five hundredth. I reached my first destination, the seven hundredth room, in under an hour.

The journey had not been without its challenges. My arms and shoulders were scraped from occasional brushes with the walls, and the corridor's swaying became more pronounced the further I went. When I steadied myself against the wall, it felt oddly soft, similar to a sponge. Testing other walls, I found they also had a soft, yielding texture, akin to rubber.

Curious, I jabbed my pencil into the wall, half-expecting it to leave a hole. When I extracted the pencil, the graphite tip remained sharp. It was clear the structure of the walls was becoming less solid this deep into the chain of replications. The floor underfoot shared this newfound malleability, and I couldn't help but wonder how much further I could go before the floor might give way. Would my next collision with a wall send me right through it?

I cautiously remounted the motorcycle, determined to continue but mindful of the risks. When I reached the eight hundredth room, an abrupt twist in the hallway unseated me. A sudden, loud impact felt as though something external had crashed into the hallway, violently jerking it to the left. To my surprise, an alien room protruded halfway into my room. This foreign entity attempted to disentangle itself but seemed stuck.

The walls of the intruding room were almost ethereal at first, but as it remained intertwined with my room, its features began to solidify, growing clearer and more tangible with each passing moment.

A New Universe

I watched in silent awe as the alien room slowly solidified, drawing from the reality of my current room. As the once ephemeral walls hardened, I retreated, fearful of being consumed or trapped by a desk or wall. Suddenly, the rooms began a violent struggle, jostling back and forth as if in a desperate attempt to break free of each other.

Reactively, I leaped onto the motorcycle, my sudden acceleration making it difficult to maintain a grip on the handlebars. A few seconds later, I crashed. When I turned back, I saw the two rooms had finally managed to extricate themselves from one another. Where a solid wall had once stood, now there was a vast expanse of nothingness.

Regaining my composure, I tentatively approached the edge of this new precipice. My curiosity propelled me to the edge, where I peered out into a universe completely unlike our own. The outside was a sea of emptiness, startlingly white, adorned only by long, snaking ribbons that pierced the void.

Closer examination revealed that these ribbons were in fact extended series of Backrooms, one copy attached to another in an endless line. I could see how the rooms gradually lost their solidity towards the ends of the ribbons, walls and furniture faded into mere outlines before disappearing completely.

Hundreds of these ribbons crisscrossed the void, some tangled in knots, some trailing off into the distance, and some broken and flying freely. I dared not lean too far over the edge, into the infinite white expanse, but it was clear that all these ribbons pointed back towards the origin I had embarked from earlier.

Our assumption that the copied rooms disintegrated when we switched off the machines each night was evidently incorrect. These strands of Backrooms continued to exist, proof of our work each day. It seemed that with the start of each machine cycle, a new ribbon of Backrooms was born.

I couldn't help but marvel at this vast, surreal universe that our experiments had inadvertently spawned. It was a hauntingly beautiful testament to our endeavors and our blunders. Our creations were not as transient as we had thought; they were part of something far larger and stranger than we could have ever imagined.

I Know Them!

Suddenly, a neighboring ribbon collided with my room, throwing me off balance and nearly pitching me into the void. I clawed my way back into the room, barely evading a solidifying wall, only to trip over a desk that had just taken form.

As I stumbled back onto my feet, a phantom-like figure started to materialize before me. It reached out to touch my arm, its hand passing through my body and leaving a trail of icy coldness. Before I could fully react, a unmaterialized knife whistled through the air, passing through my body before sticking into the wall behind me.

I spun around, coming face to face with a group of five ghostly figures that were steadily gaining solidity. Each was armed with a weapon and was closing the distance between us. Understanding that I had only a matter of seconds before they could harm me, I vaulted onto the motorcycle and gunned it.

As I roared away, a sharp pain seared through my back and warmth began to spread across it. I knew instinctively that I had been stabbed. I rode as far as I could before the pain forced me to stop. Reaching back, my hand brushed against the cold handle of the knife sticking out of my back. Darkness hovered at the edges of my vision.

By the time I made it back to the other scientists, the bleeding had stopped, but the knife remained lodged in my back. With practiced efficiency, Dr C extracted the knife and stitched up my wound, his calm demeanor belying the urgency of the situation.

As I sat recovering, I relayed my experiences to the others: the colliding ribbons, the ghostly attackers, the continued existence of the Backrooms beyond our control. They absorbed every detail, furiously scribbling notes and postulating theories to account for the bizarre phenomena.

Yet, there was one detail I kept to myself, a revelation too unnerving to share. The ghostly figures that had attacked me, they were the scientists, or rather, their copies from another Backroom. My colleagues, in some twisted and altered form, had tried to kill me. The implications of this were too horrifying to contemplate and I decided to keep this information to myself, for now.

Personal Life

I made my way home after the incident, doing my best to hide the injury from my family. My excuse of a "work-related accident" was met with skepticism, especially from my wife. Her probing questions were difficult to dodge, and the worry in her eyes was hard to ignore. I reassured her with the only promise I could give - that I would be more careful.

The extra income from the Backrooms project had allowed us to purchase a vacation home far from the city, a serene haven amid nature. My wife and our son relished in the tranquility it provided, their joy a balm to my fraying nerves. It gave me a refuge, a place where I could escape the screams and torment that echoed through the Backrooms. A place that was distant from the brutal reality of my job.

But even amidst the calm, a gnawing question lingered in the back of my mind. How long could I hold on before the nightmares I'd witnessed in the Backrooms broke my resolve? The secrets I bore were a burden I couldn't share. The faces of the Smith copies, the suffering, the ghostly figures of my colleagues - they were all locked away within me. And each day, the weight of these secrets threatened to crush me. My world was a ticking time bomb of silence and sanity, counting down to an inevitable implosion.

Playing it Safe

The fear of another ghostly encounter lingered in our minds, coloring our days with anxiety. A sense of apprehension had descended over us, altering our behavior. Now, we each had a knife hidden in our backpacks, an ever-present reminder of the unknown danger that loomed. As we descended into the Backrooms, we dared not venture beyond copy four hundred. We feared the instability of the structures that lay deeper, their potential to break off and lead us into the labyrinthine unknown.

The sounds of our home ribbon crashing into others was a constant source of alarm. Each jolt made us reach for our weapons, our eyes scanning the room for signs of an attack. But nothing came. The stability of our position, it seemed, kept us isolated from the interconnecting chaos that raged outside. But this meant progress was slow. We were stuck at a crossroads, hiding from the horrors that lay ahead and the horrific experiments that lay behind.

After weeks of stagnation, frustration overcame fear. If I couldn't wait for a breach to occur naturally, I'd have to create it. My new plan was simple and risky - I was going to use explosives. Though it took some convincing, Dr C finally conceded, and my unusual request for dynamite was granted by our military overseers.

We began at copy four hundred. Our first detonation echoed ominously through the rooms, but it left no visible mark. Undeterred, we ventured deeper, pushing the limits of our fear. Yet each explosion yielded the same results. The Backrooms, we realized, were held together by more than just the R22 machines.

But at copy six hundred, we finally achieved our breakthrough. An explosion ripped through the room, leaving a hole in the wall. We took turns peering through the aperture, our gazes meeting the vastness of the new universe. We spent days mapping the ribbons we could see, fascinated by the way they intertwined, overlapped, and detached.

Emboldened, we dared to venture deeper to copy seven hundred. Here, the rooms swayed like an unsteady ship at sea, throwing us off balance. However, this instability allowed us to create larger breaches, blowing off entire walls, floors, or ceilings to get different views of the cosmos. We could see ribbons passing by, detached yet adhering to a set schedule, akin to comets orbiting a celestial body.

But even as we ventured deeper, the origin point where the ribbons sprang from remained obscured. A few close encounters with other ribbons led us to tense moments of waiting, weapons in hand. But no attack came. It made me wonder - how many of these Backroom ribbons housed life, and how many were just echoes of existence?

Floating

My curiosity about the origin of the Backrooms became a relentless itch I could no longer ignore. One day, armed with nothing but a length of rope and a safety suit, I made a leap of faith. We had blown off a wall again, and as my colleagues secured the rope around my waist, I jumped into the new universe. To my surprise, I found myself enveloped in an atmosphere, heavy and tangible. With a reassuring thumbs-up, I signaled to my companions that I was safe. I was floating, drifting in a serene silence punctuated only by my own heartbeat.

It was an unsettling sensation, drifting outside the confines of the Backroom. But in this new environment, I found that I could navigate my way by moving my arms, much like swimming in water. I used this newfound mobility to peer over the room I had just left.

The sight of two ribbons colliding soundlessly was an unnerving spectacle. Yet, I found myself drawn to it, unable to look away from the silent, chaotic dance unfolding before my eyes.

Yet the pull of the origin was stronger. I refocused my gaze, attempting to penetrate the swirling white fog that obscured my vision. I longed for a glimpse of what lay at the heart of this universe, what tethered all these ribbons. I strained my eyes, feeling the fog was on the verge of thinning, only to be thwarted by another pulsating wave of dense white mist.

There was an almost rhythmic pattern to this, like the fog itself was the pulsating life source of this bizarre universe. Each time it nearly cleared, it faded back into a dense cloud, hiding whatever lay at the core. The origin remained an enigma, shrouded in its protective cloak of mist, eluding my quest for understanding. But that wouldn't deter me. The journey had just begun.

Flying

The calm before the storm was brief. Suddenly, a ribbon charged towards our room. The tether around my waist jerked violently as the scientists inside attempted a futile pullback. The collision was inevitable, and it was monumental. Our room was struck with such force, it nearly ripped apart, hanging precariously to its existence.

The rope slackened in my hands, signaling an abandonment of the rescue attempt. A selfish instinct of survival had overtaken the scientific camaraderie. The scientists, my companions, scrambled away, their figures retreating with panic-stricken leaps over the gaping tear created by the impact.

With the second hit, our room split in two, widening the chasm between us. Stranded on the remnant, I stretched my hand towards the other side, but the gap was just too vast to bridge.

All too soon, the rogue ribbon returned for a third strike. This time, I was at the mercy of its trajectory. The rope attached to my waist got entangled with the incoming ribbon, yanking me off my feet. The pull was so strong that it propelled me across the void, and I found myself tethered to the interloper, our violent visitor.

I inched my way closer to the ribbon, bracing myself against the surreal sensation of walking on top of a hallway. Fortunately, the collision had created a hole in the structure. My heart pounded as I lowered myself into the room, crawling into an alien space, my unexpected sanctuary.

Stranded, I looked around my new shelter. The familiar sterility of the Backrooms was comforting, but the isolation was daunting. Yet, this was my reality now, a new home in an unfamiliar ribbon, with the past one drifting farther away every passing moment.

Same Place

Inside this alternate ribbon, it was as if I had walked into a parallel reality, a version of the Backrooms where everything seemed eerily familiar yet drastically different. The room pulsed with the same droning hum of the fluorescent lights. The smell of old, recycled air filled my nostrils, the sameness of it all was oddly comforting.

However, as the ribbon continued to undulate, it felt like a ticking time bomb ready to detonate and cast me into the ethereal emptiness outside. My only chance of survival was to make my way towards the exit, wherever it may be in this alternate construct. With each step, I ventured deeper into the unknown.

Progressing through the clones of this alternate Backrooms, I began to notice oddities that set it apart from my home ribbon. At what I estimated to be copy five hundred, the familiar office furniture started transforming into something else entirely. Gone were the ergonomic chairs and orderly desks, replaced instead by imposing wooden blocks.

More alarming were the changes on the walls. The usual generic office art had given way to a chilling display. Knives, clubs, and a variety of crude weapons hung ominously where pictures of landscapes and motivational quotes should have been. It was as if I had stumbled into an armory of some brutal, primitive society.

The implications were clear and terrifying. This ribbon was not designed for conducting research or replicating office spaces. It was created for conflict, a battleground. And I, with only my wits and a tethering rope for defense, was walking right into it.

Traps

Just at the cusp of the four hundredth copy, I stumbled over a concealed tripwire. An arrow whooshed past, just missing my head, before embedding itself into the wall. I spun around, a shield and sword in hand, bracing myself for an attack. But all I could hear were hurried footsteps retreating into the distance. A chilling realization began to seep into my mind: this ribbon wasn't just a battleground, it was a trap-laden maze.

Setting up a makeshift barricade with the wooden blocks, I waited, my heart pounding in my ears. The room remained eerily quiet, the silence occasionally punctuated by the hum of fluorescent lights and the faint, far-off impacts of ribbon collisions. The attacker never returned, and eventually, I gathered the courage to push onwards.

My journey took an even darker turn when I discovered the bodies. They were identical to each other, armed with swords, and lying lifeless on the cold floor. The sight of their identical faces was chilling. Were they replicas, or perhaps alternate versions of a person from a different ribbon? An arrow protruding from one's back suggested that they had succumbed to a booby trap. A grim reminder that I was navigating a lethal labyrinth.

I had barely processed this when I was nearly skewered by a spear. Whirling around, I found myself face-to-face with another replica, his sword brandished overhead. With a primal yell, he lunged at me, but I managed to block the blow with my shield. In the ensuing chaos, my sword plunged into his side, eliciting a gut-wrenching scream. Instinctively, I kicked him back, and he stumbled off, defeated and bleeding. As he fled, I spotted a '7' scrawled across his back.

Returning to the bodies, I discovered they bore similar numbers: '4' and '3'. It struck me then that these were not random numbers; they were identifiers. It felt like some sick form of a contest or a game. I could almost visualize the scientists making bets on who would survive, watching from the safety of the first copies. Were these fights the price of freedom from this twisted reality? The thought both terrified and infuriated me.

Surprise Attack

My heart was pounding in my chest as I crept cautiously through the maze of booby-trapped corridors, but my fear didn't slow me down. But fear wasn't enough to save me from the next trap. An arrow shot out, burying itself in my shoulder. Pain lanced through me and I screamed, crumpling to the ground.

A copy emerged from the shadows, spear in hand, ready to take advantage of my predicament. Desperately, I hoisted my shield with my good arm, deflecting the spear, which splintered upon impact. He threw the useless weapon aside and pulled out a knife, advancing on me with a lethal intent.

The fight was brutal and quick. I struggled to my feet, narrowly avoiding a kick intended to keep me down. I knocked the knife out of the copy's hand with a well-placed kick, followed by another one to his groin that sent him reeling backward. Seeing my chance, I bolted, leaving the pained copy behind. He was quick, though, and I could hear his footfalls closing in.

Just as I felt the wind from a thrown knife whizzing past my head, I spotted another tripwire. With no other choice, I hurled myself forward, triggering an arrow trap. The arrow flew past my head, finding its mark in the pursuing copy. His momentum carried him forward a few more steps before he collapsed, lifeless.

I took a few more steps before the world swirled and I collapsed next to a water fountain, the pain from my shoulder too much to bear. My last memory before passing out was the agonizing sensation of ripping the arrow from my shoulder.

When I woke up, pain was my only companion. My shoulder throbbed with each heartbeat, but the burning thirst in my throat was even more unbearable. I forced myself to press the fountain button, the shock of cold water jolting my injured finger with unexpected pain. I drank until I was no longer thirsty, the pain in my finger now reduced to a dull throb. Looking down, I saw the fresh blood welling up from the cut.

But my shoulder was the real issue. The makeshift bandage I crafted from my torn shirt barely covered the wound, but it would have to do. It was either this, or bleed out in this madhouse of a ribbon. The choice was clear: survive.

How Many More

Every step was a fight against the pain radiating from my shoulder and throbbing in my finger, but I pushed onward. The rooms were changing, the buzzing yellow lights gave way to a clear, white glow. The rooms seemed normal, aside from the weaponry strewn about and the odd number scrawled on the walls.

My heart pounded in my chest with the knowledge that I was getting closer to the end. Any remaining copies could be my downfall, given my weakened state. I stuck to knives and my shield; my wounded shoulder would not be much use swinging a sword.

As I limped forward, I came across more casualties of this strange copy battleground. Copies numbered 2 and 5 lay lifeless, victims of a lethal spear fight. Near the exit door, I found copies 1 and 10, both fell victim to the treacherous door traps.

Every step was an ordeal. My finger throbbed in rhythm with my heartbeats, its dark blue color was a grim indicator of my condition. Yet, my predicament was about to take an unexpected turn.

The sounds of conflict reached my ears, harsh shouts echoing through the Backroom corridors. I inched closer, spotting two copies hiding behind barricades of wooden blocks near the exit. One would hurl a knife or spear, while the other retorted with a barrage of insults. A stalemate.

My mind raced, unsure of how they'd react if they spotted me. Would they unite to take me down? A flash of inspiration hit me - I still had one stick of dynamite left.

With shaky hands, I lit the fuse and waited, each tick of the clock an agonizing eternity. At the last possible moment, I hurled it into the room and took cover, hoisting my shield protectively. The explosion that followed was deafening, two piercing screams echoing in the blast.

I ran into the room, knives at the ready, but it was unnecessary. Nothing was left of the two copies. The blast had done its job. My entire body ached from the shockwave, my ears bleeding. But the path ahead was clear. The end was near. I just had to keep moving.

A Year Lost

The door to the exit swung open abruptly. Strong hands grabbed me, pulling me from the battle-worn rooms of the Backrooms and into the bustling reality of the laboratory. A throng of scientists, some familiar, some new, surrounded me. Their expressions a mix of shock, relief, and awe.

"I didn't think we'd ever see you again," Dr. C said. He had an older look about him. His once jet-black hair was now sprinkled with grays, his face lined with the stress of a year I was absent from.

A year.

The word hung in the air, heavy as a stone. I had been missing for an entire year. I scanned the faces of the other scientists. They nodded, their solemn faces confirming the unimaginable truth. It seemed like an instant to me, but I had jumped an entire year in time when I crossed over to the other ribbon.

They filled me in on all that had transpired during my absence. The new experiments, the breakthroughs, the setbacks, the terror they felt when they couldn't find me, the relief when I was spotted emerging from the Backrooms. It was a lot to process, a whole year's worth of life condensed into a rushed conversation.

Fear was palpable amongst the team. They had seen what I had been through. The dangers of the deep copies, the monstrous clones, the threat of losing oneself in time, everything. This knowledge had dampened their boldness, making them cautious about delving deeper into the Backrooms.

Yet, the spark of discovery still burned in their eyes. The revelation that time travel was possible by jumping from one Backrooms to another, however dangerous, opened a whole new dimension of exploration.

The Smiths, I was told, were especially intrigued. As they prepared for their next round of experiments, I could only imagine what was to come, knowing full well the risks and potential that lay ahead. But for now, my job was to heal and adjust to a world that had moved on a year without me.

Homecoming

Walking through the door to my own home was nothing short of a shock for my wife. Seeing me appear out of the blue, after a year of my inexplicable absence, was too much to bear. Her eyes widened, her complexion paled, and she crumpled onto the floor, unconscious. I was, to her, a ghost returning from the abyss of the unknown.

Our son, Everett, looked up at me with innocent, questioning eyes. "Stranger," he pronounced, pointing a chubby finger at me. His word was like a dagger to my heart. My own son didn't recognize me. I felt a lump in my throat, and tears welled up in my eyes. Overwhelmed by a rush of emotions, I broke down and cried.

The next day brought a surprise visitor to our doorstep. A military car pulled up, and a Smith in full uniform emerged, carrying a box. He handed it to me with a solemn look, his eyes betraying no emotion.

Inside the box, nestled among packing peanuts, was my favorite coffee cup and the microphone that Dr. C and I had used to cheat on the trivia game. Those old artifacts brought a sad smile to my face. They were remnants of a different time, a different reality, memories of a year lost.

Among those mementos, there was an envelope. It was a stark reminder of the world I had left behind, the classified realm I had navigated for so long. My top-secret agreement was enclosed, a stark reminder of the potential lifetime in jail if I ever breathed a word about the Backrooms.

But attached to that threatening piece of paper was something unexpected. A check, substantial enough to ensure a comfortable retirement. The monetary compensation was a silent agreement between the Smiths and me. A tacit understanding that the secrets of the Backrooms would remain secrets.

It was a simple trade-off: silence for security. My lips were sealed. My bank account, on the other hand, was now pleasantly overflowing.

1 Year Later

The nightmares linger, an unfortunate residue of my time spent in the Backrooms. They were horrific, a collage of the countless tests and the anguished screams of the duplicates. A perpetual echo of torment that reverberated in my skull long after I'd awakened. Each time, the question remained: how many more years could I persist in the belief that they were merely copies, a convenient illusion to mask the disturbing truth? I was afraid that, sooner or later, this metaphorical wall would crumble and my sanity would follow suit.

My days were spent with Everett, my son. His presence was a balm to the wounds left by the Backrooms. However, a worrying trend had started to appear in his behavior. Each day, he would engross himself in drawing what he called "long squiggly worms" flying across the sky. An eerie sense of déjà vu washed over me every time I glanced at his sketches. The last time I'd seen something akin to this was in the Backrooms, where the vast expanse of the alien universe was teeming with those terrifying ribbons. Was it possible? Could Everett be visualizing the same ribbons that haunted my nightmares?

I found myself routinely passing by my old workplace, the facility where the gateway to the Backrooms was situated. It seemed to be buzzing with more activity each day; cars were constantly pulling in and out, while the number of guards had seemingly doubled. I couldn't help but wonder about the sheer number of Smiths that had passed through those ominous doorways since I left. Did they too carry the weight of the Backrooms with them, or were they blissfully unaware of the horrors that lurked beyond the veil of reality?

2 Years Later

Two years on from the Backrooms experiment and my mental fortitude eventually buckled under the weight of suppressed memories. The nightmares seeped into my waking life, culminating in a hospital admission that lasted for an agonizing month. My daily routine was now punctuated by a plethora of medication; my breakfast a kaleidoscope of pills that were supposed to keep my demons at bay.

To cope, I started attending therapy sessions. There, I danced around the truth, offering bits and pieces of my experience without ever really unveiling the whole horrific picture. How could I, when the full disclosure would mean a lifetime in jail?

Meanwhile, Everett's obsession with the flying worms in the sky persisted. Day after day, he'd sketch them with an unsettling fervor, his little fingers moving almost feverishly across the paper. On a whim, I asked him if he saw them in the clouds, hoping to finally make some sense of his drawings. He simply shook his head, insisting that the clouds merely hid them from view.

One day, as we were standing outside, he stretched his arm and pointed towards the city. The direction of his pointed finger chilled me to the bone - he was pointing at my former workplace, the starting point of his imagined worms. Could it be a mere coincidence, or was he somehow glimpsing the unseen threads of the Backrooms universe? The thought of it sent shivers down my spine.

5 Years Later

Five years on, therapy remained a constant in my life. She prescribed me a potent sleeping pill potent enough to knock out a horse. Every morning, I woke up in a disorienting haze, the room spinning around me. One day, in my stupor, I made a rush for the bathroom, only to crash into the wall. As I lay there on the floor, a throbbing knee and a wet pair of pants, I couldn't help but think of the utter absurdity of it all.

A week later, my knee had swelled to twice its size. Frustrated and concerned, my wife took me to the doctor's office. What should have been a simple diagnosis turned into a perplexing riddle. The first x-ray of my knee was inexplicably faint, just a ghostly outline that was barely discernible. The subsequent ones yielded the same, puzzling results, each image revealing nothing but an ethereal shape.

The unsettling realization hit me like a freight train - I was a COPY!, a fabrication of the original. The walls of my sanity crumbled yet again, this time under the weight of this newfound knowledge. I felt like a stranger in my own skin, a foreign entity born in the Backrooms, now lost in a world where I didn't belong.

The questions came pouring in, each more daunting than the last. Was this Dr C's plan all along? Was I a mere lab rat in his twisted experiment? What happened to the original me? I recalled my watch breaking during the initial experiment - did it symbolize the original me being pulled into the Backrooms, replaced by a mere echo?

My mind was a whirlwind of confusion, teetering on the brink of insanity. The truth was harsh, and no amount of medication could cushion its brutal impact.

10 Years Later

Ten years later, my existential crisis was a constant companion, questioning my identity every waking moment. I had thoughts, memories, and feelings. Wasn't that enough to be human? Yet, my son Everett was developing an inexplicable connection to the Backrooms. Could my origin, as a copy, have gifted him this uncanny ability to perceive the elusive ribbons?

Despite the urge to flee, a magnetic force seemed to tether me to the Backrooms, the eerie place of my birth. As I became less corporeal, the bond with the Backrooms seemed to grow stronger, an ironic mockery of existence. Just as my faint x-ray images suggested, I was slowly phasing out of existence, the life force that constituted my being was draining away. From the onset of this degeneration, I had roughly a month before I would completely vanish.

Reluctantly, I involved Everett, my only compass to the Backrooms. One morning, we ventured into the city and waited for a ribbon to appear. When Everett detected one, he guided me towards it, sketching a rough map. As I stood in the exact spot Everett pointed out, I felt an infusion of energy, a breath of life, returning to me. As my energy replenished, the stark reality of the Backrooms started materializing around me - the walls, pictures, desk, and a charging Smith.

I was slammed against the wall, the air forcefully driven out of my lungs. Gasping for breath, I watched in horror as the Smith raised a club to strike me down. But then, to my astonishment, he collapsed, a knife protruding from his back. Everett stood there, the innocence in his eyes replaced by a fearful determination.

The distant shout of another Smith broke the eerie silence. Everett helped me up, leading me through several copies of the Backrooms while tracing his hands on the walls. Suddenly, he shouted, "Here it is!" and pushed against the wall. A door opened into our world. Before I could react, Everett shoved me out. His fascination with the

Backrooms was palpable, but I couldn't let him stay. Just as I pulled him through, another Smith burst out of the door and charged into the alley, never looking back.

I hastily closed the door after absorbing a final surge of energy, a last connection to my origins. Witnessing the longing on Everett's face, I made a vow - he would never step into the Backrooms again.

20 Years Later

I'm a grandpa! My son Everett has a cute daughter named Alexia, she is the most beautiful thing that has ever happened in my life. Fast forward to twenty years later, I was blessed with the title of a grandfather. Alexia, my granddaughter, was a sparkling beam of joy and sanity in my life. I cherished her deeply, and she served as my anchor, my hope against the perpetual haunting of the Backrooms. Everett, however, continued to wrestle with his uncanny connection to that eerie world. I sensed it was only a matter of time before it lured him back into its relentless clutches.

To stave off our gradual fading, Everett had discovered certain hotspots in the city that emanated the Backroom's energy, not directly within a ribbon. We frequented these spots weekly, replenishing ourselves. I noticed others who were drawn to these spots. I often wondered if they were more copies like me, inexplicably drawn by the Backrooms' enigmatic pull.

One day, a familiar stranger sought me out. She introduced herself as the daughter of one of my fellow scientists, but she was not the original—she was a copy. Her tale was tragic. She had died in a car accident, and her distraught father, one of my old colleagues, had used the Backrooms to bring her back to life. I immediately recognized her resemblance to Dr. C, the only other person with the knowledge to operate the machines.

I learned that Dr. C had passed away, leaving me with a lingering question—who now wielded the power of the machines? This woman, the living testament of Dr. C's desperate love, revealed her mission. She had traced other copies and urged me to pen down my experiences as a warning for others.

If you are reading this journal, know this—the Backrooms are a realm of endless torment and suffering. Its siren call attempts to lure us back every day. I fear the day when my resolve shatters, pulling me back into its twisted existence. I'm driven by an urgent mission to sever its ties with our world, to shield my son and granddaughter from its insidious grasp. I had initially believed that the R22 machines birthed the Backrooms, but now I understand—they merely unchained a monster.

9 798223 453314